SAN ANTONIO MISSION

AMID THE VASTNESS
OF ALL ELSE SAGA
BOOK FIVE

SAN ANTONIO MISSION

C.S. HUMBLE

SHORTWAVE
PUBLISHING

Cover and interior design by Alan Lastufka.

First Shortwave Edition published August 2025.

10 9 8 7 6 5 4 3 2 1

ISBN 978-1-959565-70-3 (Paperback)
ISBN 978-1-959565-71-0 (eBook)

Amid the Vastness of All Else Saga

That Light Sublime Trilogy

Book 1 – The Massacre at Yellow Hill

Book 2 – A Red Winter in the West

Book 3 – The Light of a Black Star

The Peregrine Estate Trilogy

Book 4 – To Carry a Body to Its Resting Place

Book 5 – San Antonio Mission

Book 6 – The Baroness of the Eastern Seaboard

For Josh Rountree

One of Texas's greatest literary sons.

ABOARD THE *P.W. WARMACK TEXAS TRAILRUNNER* EN ROUTE FROM ABILENE TO SAN ANTONIO

By way of train, via a ticket purchased in Abilene, Texas, Gilbert Ptolemy traveled the iron road toward San Antonio. He sat, newspaper in one hand, looking out the window of the barber car. The locomotive, billowing smoke from its black, conical stack, thundered over the night-swept plain. A silver-dollar moon burned big and bright, its beams coloring grass and tree and limb and leaf and rolling landscape to white. As if all the world had died with the falling sun, and all that remained was the spirit of all that had been.

Snip-snip-snip went the barber's scissors and yack-yack-yack went the barber himself. "You ever been to San Antonio?" Cyrus asked the white, dapper-looking dandy sitting in the chair, never slowing down. "I got a brother there, married to a hateful woman. Got six kids, fifty acres, and a pile of headaches for all that settlin' down bullshit is worth."

If there were opinionless barbers in the world, Ptolemy had never met one.

Snip-snip-snip went Cyrus, on and on. Then he leaned closer, bowing his spine to examine his work. "I thought about doin' it myself, you know."

"Oh yeah?" asked the dandy. He was pale as milk, black-haired with a bushy mustache.

"Make my way to someplace pretty with an even prettier woman. Buy her expensive clothes, perfume. Give her my attention. All the things pretty girls like."

Ptolemy grinned, shaking his head, and went back to the newspaper, half reading and half listening. He couldn't have been less interested in the idea of marriage.

The dandy piped up. "You ever find one worth settling down with?"

The barber drew his hands back and looked up, as if all the memories of his life were writ in a long scrawl along the ceiling trim. "You know, come to think of it, I believe I did." He cocked his head to the side and smiled. "Rosemary."

"Pretty?"

"Oh, sure," he said. "Well, pretty as they get

for those willing to consider a fella like me. But I signed up to fight in the war, and she went off to California. Believe she married a saloon owner. Yeah. I figure Rosemary was the one put on God's green Earth for me, and I missed my chance. Damn shame."

Mention of the war, unlike marriage, piqued Ptolemy's interest considerably. Without looking away from the newspaper, he asked, "Which side?"

"Which side of what?" Cyrus said. "California?"

"Which side in the war?" Ptolemy stared over the edge of the newspaper.

Cyrus swallowed hard, his gaze sliding to Ptolemy's gunbelt then back to the Black man's eyes. "Jesus, mister, ain't no need to give a man like me a look like that. Hell, I was one of the first to sign up with the Army of the Ohio. I'm as abolitionist as they come, sir." He returned to his labor. *Snip-snip-snip, snip-snip-snip.*

"Ow," the dandy snapped. "Fuckin' watch the ears, goddamn it."

"My apologies." The barber took a big breath and wiped a damp, trembling hand across his brow.

"Hellfire," said the dandy, checking the rim of one ear in the mirror. "No need to ruffle feathers, friend. Damn war is over," he said, not even bothering to give Ptolemy a look. "Y'all got what you wanted. As memory serves, what was it? Last month or some such they declared in Texas—Granger's proclamation. Emancipation Day some call it. I say, good for ya. Let bygones be bygones. Equal to equal. Like unto self-same like."

Ptolemy let the tented newspaper fall over, where it folded against his knees. "Bygones," he said, his voice cold as ice.

"Aw, now, come on, mister," said the dandy. "Don't get sour. I didn't mean nothing by it."

Ptolemy stood up, letting the newspaper slip to the floor.

Cyrus, self-proclaimed veteran of the Union army, showed the worth of his courage and the truth of his claim when he stepped back three paces from the two other men.

"What's your name?" asked Ptolemy.

"I'll take yours first, stranger, before I give you mine," said the man as he pushed himself out of the barber chair. On his hips was a left-handed gun belt, where a revolver hung heavy in the crossdraw fashion. The dandy drew himself up to his full height, rolled his shoulders back, and set his head to lean in annoyance, waiting.

Ptolemy almost laughed. He was a head taller than the dandy, easy, and fifty pounds heavier. Every single ounce of that was corded muscle over bones dense as a mule's. And his reach was very long. Long enough to snatch the dandy up by the scruff of the neck and let him dangle there like an angry pup. "Name's Gilbert Ptolemy," he said, squeezing his hand into a fist so tight that every weathered knuckle cracked. If the little man ran his mouth, he'd get a fat lip. And if he went for his gun, Ptolemy would knock him down, as he had so many like him before, and stomp a mudhole into his chest.

The dandy's eyes were cool hazel pools with little yellow rings that shimmered gold in the oil lamps' light. He looked at Ptolemy, entirely unafraid, and smiled. It was a strange kind of smile, a stretched frown that lifted on one side yet drooped on the other. "I assure you, Mr. Ptolemy, that if my words gave offense, it was entirely unintended. My name is Oliver Maine, and by your posture and sneering and fist-knotting, I feel obliged to tell you that I am a member of the Gunfighters Guild. Of the twenty-five members numbered among the fastest draws in these United States, I am the Four. I'm on my way to San Antonio to claim the Three, and I assure you sir—with all due respect—that if you make for violence in this room, your life will be sped toward oblivion at the low cost of a single bullet you'll never even see fired."

Ptolemy stared at Maine. Maine stared back. Their gazes coiled like two prize fighters slithering for dominance in the clinch, each man silent in his total appraisal of the other's inexorable self. A few breaths passed. Many more heart beats.

"Big claim," said Ptolemy.

"I am many things, sir," the gunfighter said as he drew back the red, satin cloth of his brocade vest. Beneath, pinned to the strap of his overalls, was a little silver icon. A simple etching of the number four shone. "But you will find neither a bluff nor liar among them."

"Jesus Christ," said Cyrus, clutching his scissors close to his chest. "Listen, sir, I'm awful sorry about clipping your ear—"

"It'll mend," the man said, still looking at Ptolemy. "Though, if Mr. Ptolemy here does what his face tells me he wants to do, the wound I give him certainly will not."

Ptolemy slowly relaxed his fist so that his fingers dangled heavy, throbbing in anticipation. Sure, he was a fast draw, but he certainly wasn't in a rush to test that against a goddamn professional gunfighter. And besides, he had important business to attend to in San Antonio. But more than those things—more important than anything the world or society or culture wagered in that moment—there was Carson to think about.

His son.

"Well, at least you sounded fancy in your threatening, Mr. Maine," said Ptolemy, relaxing at the shoulders. "Never met a member of the Guild who didn't love to put filigree on a goddamn ultimatum."

"Never miss a chance to do so," said Maine, extending his hand. "Again, my apologies for the offense I gave. I spoke poorly where I should have kept my thoughts to myself."

Ptolemy shook the man's hand. "It's not your speaking-up that I took issue with, Mr. Maine. It is the ignorance in your opinion."

Maine squeezed his hand firmly. "Let me finish my haircut, then you will educate my opinion with your own position. I will meet you in the bar car. You will talk. I will listen. We will drink."

Ptolemy squeezed back to meet Maine's strength. "And you'll pay."

Oliver Maine laughed, that frowning smile returning. "Happily."

They did exactly as the gunfighter had suggested. Ptolemy talked a long time over the rumbling train's powerful wheels, sipping at his bourbon between thoughts.

Maine said little, mostly listening as he had promised, his hazel eyes rarely breaking contact with Ptolemy's.

"There can be no bygones between former slave to the former master," said Ptolemy. "Perhaps the great grandchildren of these two cultures can find equity among them, but for our generation, with hundreds of years yoked in bondage in our recent memories, you will find no measure of willingness to compromise. No hope of forgiveness. God is trying to teach me to forgive, but I am a stubborn learner."

Maine nodded. "Consider my opinion transformed, Mr. Ptolemy. Tell me, what takes you to San Antonio. You know my business there already."

The gunfighter's seemingly lazy confidence and easy way impressed Ptolemy, and so he entrusted him with a greater portion of the truth than a lie. "My employer, a cattleman, has asked that I attend to business on his behalf. There is a group of freed peoples recently released by a ranching landowner—Lieutenant Colonel Leslie Gramm. Gramm has a cruel and vengeful reputation. Meaning, my employer believes Gramm will be furious at being forced to release them, which puts them in immediate danger. He knows they can never trust a White man again, so he asked me, his proxy, to come in his stead."

"He must place a great deal of trust in you," said Maine.

"And I in him. He bids me to make an offer of fair wage and treatment for their services. So, here I am, on my way to San Antonio to hire these men and drinking with, allegedly," said Ptolemy with a smirk, "the fourth-fastest gunhand alive. Color me surprised."

Maine lifted his glass. "Fourth in pin only, Mr. Ptolemy. I assure you, with my left hand I am the equal of every gunfighter in the world. With my right I am their superior." He sipped.

"You guildfolk are always sayin' that," said Ptolemy. "Never met one of you who didn't think they were the One. You all see it as a matter of time, until your time is up."

Maine tilted his head, his cold eyes flashing with confidence. "However many guildfolk you think are delusional, you can subtract one from that."

"You being the subtraction, I take it."

"You take it correctly," said Maine.

Ptolemy had to laugh. The man's confidence was unshakable. "You really believe that."

"I have to."

"Met a fella in Arizona a while back, maybe six months ago, who said the same. The number Seven. Name was—"

"Two-Pistol Thomas Longfellow," said Maine.

"Yeah, saw him take the Six. Smoothest draw I've ever seen. You know him?"

Maine leveled his cool eyes at him. "Met him three months ago. Our relationship did not last long."

"Oh," said Ptolemy. "Well, that's a shame. He seemed nice enough."

Maine shifted, tapped the bar, and ordered

another round. "Tell me, will your business in San Antonio allow you the time to accompany me to my own appointment? Among my braggart vices, I confess, I am also a showman."

Ptolemy considered the man and the fondness growing between them, but then the requirements of his mission. He shook his head. "The sands of my life are my own, but my family is the hourglass. I've got to be back to Abilene as quick as I'm able. My boy is there. He's prone to get melancholy if I'm away from him for too long."

"Why did he not accompany you? See the world with his father."

"He too looks like you. I took him as my own after a mutual calamity drew us together. Experience has taught me that traveling with him raises the hackles of the ignorant fucks populating this country. So, he's working on the ranch, and I think it'll do him some good to be without me for a piece. I'm guessing you ain't got a family."

The bartender poured them another round.

The gunfighter sipped his whiskey, then ran his tongue over his teeth, sucking lightly. "Had one," he said. "Scarlet fever took them. Tried to take me too, but I refused it. Town sawbones, Doc Tanner, came upon our home, making the rounds as respite from the pestilence tent where the sick were laid to either recover or die.

I don't remember it much, but Tanner claimed he found me clinging to my daughter's dead body for dear life. Pried me away from her and took me under his care, where I proved too stout for the Reaper Man. I, like so many widowers surviving the fever, regained my strength, grieved, and cursed God. And now I am wholly bent on testing Death every day for what he took, all while gaining the notoriety and fortune that comes with being better than any living person with this." He tapped the bottom of his glass on the butt of his revolver grip.

Ptolemy nodded. "I'm sorry for your loss. Here's to many more victories against Ol' Grim." He clinked his glass against Maine's.

The gunfighter smiled over the top of the whiskey glass. "Most foolish thing Death ever did was to make an enemy of me."

The train whistle blew. Outside, the ghost of the world floated by, losing its speed, a white shroud presiding over all.

The car attendant, topped in a red felt hat, stepped through the doorway, slid it shut behind him, and called out, "San Marcos stop. Stop for San Marcos. Last stop before San Antonio. Thirty minutes."

Ptolemy rubbed his tired face. "It's been a pleasure, but I'm off to bed. Gotta get some sleep before duty calls."

Maine stood up and extended a hand. "Gilbert Ptolemy, was it?"

They shook. "Yes," he said.

"Good luck with hiring those hands," said Maine, his eyes drifting for a moment before the came back to meet Ptolemy's. "You're right to hurry back to your boy. My deepest regard and hopes to you both."

"And good luck with those hands of yours too, Mr. Maine."

* * *

The next morning, Ptolemy awoke to the howl of a train whistle. The Texas sun, yellow as an apricot, streamed through the window hot on his face. The locomotive groaned, then whined to full stop as Ptolemy squinted against the light, head throbbing. He pushed himself up, smoothed his clothes, and exited the train. Not knowing why, he found himself scanning the departing hoard of travelers for any sign of Maine. The gunfighter was not among them.

Dust blown up from the wind and foot traffic of people and cattle threw a haze across stone buildings, grocers, vendors and the three-story limestone walls of the Alamo Mission. The mission itself, bleached by a hundred and more years in the pestilential sun, stood a ruinous grave marker before the grassless thoroughfare.

Ptolemy checked the time: mid-morning. The streets were stuffed with bonneted ladies accompanied by foppish young men. A black-haired Mexican woman, a grand smile upon her face, happily swayed in a skirt of gold and green and blue between a vegetable stand and the small overstacked cart that bore the little cornucopia of her harvest. Gun-toting cowboys of all colors pushed short herds of beef and dairy cattle toward empty stock cars. The wind blew sand and the scent of manure through it all.

Near the center of town, Ptolemy found a telegraph station close by the Moore Street Hotel. A slight, blond man of middling years clerked the counter, shuffling through papers. The attendant did not look up when he said, "Sending or receiving?"

"Both," said Ptolemy.

The man rifled through the leaves of paper, slipping one over the other, acutely focused on their organization. "Sender?"

The door whined open on its hinges behind him, but Ptolemy did not look back.

"Judge Hezekiah Ellison, by way of Abilene."

"And your name, sir?" he asked, entirely disinterested.

"Why I believe that man there is the infamous Gilbert Ptolemy," came the voice of a woman.

He did not recognize the voice and turned to

examine the newcomer. The woman, shorter than him by a head-and-a-half, with dark skin and a curved, imperfect smile bright as a slice of moonlight, appraised him with hazelnut eyes. When they shifted, they caught the light and ignited to amber. Her black hair, banded with a leather cord, was pulled tight at the scalp before it flared back wild as a dandelion puff.

He did not know this woman, and part of him suddenly felt cheated that life had waited until this moment to present the opportunity.

"I am Ptolemy," he said. "Though infamous may be too strong an appraisal. You are?"

"Sarah Lockhart. As you are with the Judge, so am I."

He knew the phrase—one of the many key phrases used among agents of the Judge. It meant they could be trusted. "Heard of you," he said. "Though. . . no one said—"

"Said what of me, Mr. Ptolemy?" She tilted her head playfully.

"Mr. Ptolemy," said the clerk, officiously interrupting. "Your telegram, sir."

He turned to see the clerk holding an envelope pinched between two fingers so that the flat yellow of it shined like a gold bar in the sunlight.

Ptolemy reached for it. "Thank you."

The clerk drew back. "One dollar, sir."

"*A dollar?* For what?"

"Oh," said Sarah Lockhart, smirking. "Are you a little short?"

Ptolemy turned back, almost angry, then almost laughing. "What? No. I'm not short on anything, I just—" He turned back to the clerk. "Why am I paying to receive a telegram that has already been paid for?"

"Transmission fee, sir."

"A do-fuckin' what now?"

"No need for that, sir. I don't make the policies. I just have to enforce them as the telegrapher and clerk officer."

"*Clerk officer?*" Ptolemy thought about slapping the gold-rimmed glasses off the man's face. "What in the hell is this place?"

Sarah stepped forward and patted Ptolemy on the shoulder. "Easy, big fella. Let me help."

"I certainly do not need any help—"

Sarah ignored him, set her elbows on the clerk's counter, and leaned her weight forward. "You'll have to pardon my friend; he doesn't really speak the complicated yet primitive language of extortion."

The clerk drew back, offended. "*Extortion?* Ma'am, I am simply operating by the measure of—"

"Listen, sugar. I'm sure you make a nice little side amount on your, what did you call it?"

The clerk slipped into nervousness. "It's not

me that's making anything on the transmission—"

"Transmission fee. Right. Okay, well, I have a receiving fee when it comes to telegrams, and it just so happens that I also charge exactly one American dollar. So why don't you just give me the telegram, and we'll call it. . ." Using a finger, she drew an invisible square.

The clerk swallowed, unsure. "But it's not addressed to you."

"I have his proxy."

"His what?"

"I. . . have," Sarah said, tilting her head to each shoulder to punctuate every word, "his. . . proxy." She looked back over her shoulder at Gilbert. "Don't I, Mr. Ptolemy?"

Ptolemy smiled, shaking his head. Who in the hell was this woman, was all he could think, and "She does," was all he could say.

"See?" Sarah said to the dumbfounded clerk. "Now, I'll take that telegram. Or I'll be obliged to take every cent of my receiving fee out of your ass."

"There's no need to get mean about it," said the clerk.

"That's yet to be seen." She extended the flat of her palm.

Outside the office, Ptolemy and Sarah made their way along the sidewalk. Sarah began opening the telegram as Ptolemy said, "The Judge didn't say anything about sending someone else."

"Sure he did. Says it right here. *G.P.*—I'm assuming that's you—*you will be obliged to meet Ms. Sarah Lockhart*—which is without question me—*at the Moore Street Hotel. You will recognize her by her unrivaled intellect and indescribable beauty and...*"

Ptolemy laughed, playfully annoyed, and snatched the telegram from her hands.

"Hey!"

"You're something else, you know it?"

"You don't know the half of it," she answered, telling him something he had already guessed.

Ptolemy stopped along the walkway, lifting the telegram closer to read it. He felt the woman's eyes on him, and, for a moment, he focused on that more than the words, keeping his chest high and his shoulders erect. Almost without knowing why, he wanted to impress her. Wanted to do all that he could to keep her looking. Out of the corner of his vision, where the outline of her beauty could be hazily seen in the late-morning light, he watched her watching him.

"Well, what's the rest of it say?" she asked.

He finally focused on the telegram. The

words were a thief to his sudden delight. "Son of a bitch," he said.

"Goddamn it. What's it say?"

He read the second portion of the telegram's contents aloud. "*Be advised: received word that the emancipated hands have fled. Taking refuge at Concepción Mission, 3 miles S. of San Ant. Make all haste.*"

"Former owner ran them off," said Sarah, a sudden venom in her voice.

"Or they escaped," said Ptolemy, "and ran for their lives."

"My horse is just across the way," said Sarah, gesturing at the hotel. "Yours?"

"Don't have one at the moment."

Sarah shook her head, looking at him incredulous. "You came to San Antonio without a way to get around?"

"Judge has a stableman here—a friend of mine who sells him a lot of horses. I'm going that way now."

"What happened to your last horse?"

"It's a long story we don't have time for. Come on."

They strode quickly out into the dusty thoroughfare, pushing past the bonneted buyers and their paramours, the bustling cowboys, and all the torrent of life washing through San Antonio. Westward clouds rolled over the sky, secretly roaming unto those indeterminable places they seek when every human eye ignores their movement.

J.J.'s Livery Stable was no more than fifteen-minutes' walk from the telegraph office. The small pine building that was the front office was attached to a three-story stable. Just below the stable's open hayloft, stuffed with sacks of feed and bales wrapped tight as a corseted Buffalo Gal, was a large dirt riding pen fenced in by whitewashed timber beams. Ptolemy was headed for the office door when from inside came the sound of two men raising their voices. Their muffled argument grew louder.

Ptolemy looked at Sarah, who gave a half laugh with her palms up.

The door flew open, and a man came spilling out, bent at the waist and hands flailing, his white straw hat flipping into the dirt. He would have gone face-first to the ground if Ptolemy hadn't caught him.

"Easy," said Ptolemy. "You alright?"

"Why that no-good son of a goat can't just. . ." The man regained his balance and looked up, revealing what might have been the most sour-looking face Ptolemy had ever seen. It was red as a pepper with watery blue eyes set into deep sockets. Little whips of brown hair floated over his bald head. His mouth was thin, sucking his lips like he'd just whacked himself on the thumb with a hammer, ready to cuss. "Why," he said, almost breathless, "thank you, sir. Name's Cid Smith." Then he turned back to the open doorway of the office and let his rage burn as white and hot as that sweaty eggshell head of his. "Jerry!"

Ptolemy followed the man's holler, looking toward the empty doorway.

"Jerry! Damn your eyes and your hands, and damn every horse you've ever bred or broken. Goddamn, penny-pinching, horse-screwing. . ." The man went on and on, cussing and raving as he pushed away from Ptolemy and went to collect his hat. "You promised that mare to me, by God," he screamed, blasting the air, "and I'm gonna make sure that everybody in town knows that Jerry Johnson is no longer an upstanding man of his own goddamn word."

"I think he gets the point, mister," said Sarah. "I believe the whole damn town got it."

"Well," said the man, breathless and slapping the dust off his black hat, "I hope they damn well do. I hope every single person from here to Austin can goddamn well hear me! Huh? You hear that Jerry? I'm gonna say it to every person I know, and soon enough you'll be out of business and a pauper to boot!"

And with that, flush with rage, the man tipped his hat to Sarah and gave a stiff nod to Ptolemy. But just as he turned to make his way out into the world, ready to waylay all humanity with the story of how Jerry Johnson was the worst horse trader that ever was or ever would be, the stable master came striding out of the office.

Skinny as a fence post and six foot six if he was an inch, Jerry Johnson was a towering wraith of a man. Seeing him come walking out of the dark of that office was like watching the cold visage of death step out among the living. His cold gray eyes peered out from under long tangles of ashy hair, considering Cid for a moment, then he lifted a single finger to point at the expanse of San Antonio beyond. "Go on," he said with a high tenor voice that did not match the man one bit. In many ways it cut right through the man's menacing appearance.

"I'm goin'!"

"Good. Because next time I'll do more than just toss your little—" His eyes had drifted to Ptolemy, and a smile the color of limestone lit his face. "My good Lord," he said. "My good and loving Lord in all of Heaven, is that Gilbert Ptolemy I see standing before me."

"J.J.," said Ptolemy in greeting.

"I hope you fucking die," said Cid, going on and on.

"Alright, that's plenty of that," said Sarah, who then drew her pistol and fired a round into the air.

"Christ almighty!" Cid howled and took off running back toward Main Street.

Johnson threw a long arm around Ptolemy's shoulder, squeezed. "It's good to see you. And who is this beautiful woman?"

Sarah used the barrel of her revolver to tip her hat to him.

"Gilbert," said Johnson, mocking astonishment. "Did you go and get married?"

"What?" The question was more a sound than a word.

Johnson shook his head slowly from side to side. "And you didn't invite me."

Sarah laughed and, to Ptolemy's shock, wrapped her arms around his waist and squeezed him tight as a lover. "The baby will be here any day."

"Oh, the hell to all this," said Ptolemy, shoving them both away.

Sarah laughed again. And he heard it for what it was: the unmistakable sound of uncomplicated delight. And quickly, so quickly, it became a sound he would want to hear forever, on and on, without ever really understanding why. He was a man who knew a great deal about himself but not much else outside of his occupation. And now, among those things about himself, he knew that this woman was creating a meridian in his life. The time before that laughter, and all the time there would be after.

Sarah introduced herself to Johnson and told him how she and Ptolemy had met. As she relayed the Judge's telegram, the gaunt stableman's gaiety surrendered to a grim seriousness.

"I know Concepción Mission," he said. "It's not too far from here. You'll both be needing a horse and tack, I figure."

"Just him," said Sarah, quicker than Ptolemy could speak. "He figures you're going to give him a good deal, but judging from what I just saw—"

"Cid's a notorious loud-mouth asshole who's too dumb to pour piss out of a boot, and too cheap to buy the boot to piss in," said Johnson, turning to walk toward the riding pen. "He offered half of what my mare is worth. I can't wait to tell everyone in town that I sold it to you for even less than his offer. Folks at the Jolene Bean will get a real kick out of that."

"I'm willing to pay full price," said Ptolemy, following him.

Johnson opened the pen gate for them. "I wouldn't dream of it. Hell, seeing as what you did for Callie. . ."

"Just trying to help," said Ptolemy.

"You did a hell of a lot more than help." Johnson led them into the open stable.

Sarah let out a low hum. "Callie your wife? Daughter?"

"Don't have one of either of those, but she's my lady, yes, ma'am."

"Well," said Sarah walking behind the two men between the rows of American quarter horses, paints, mustangs, and a lonely looking roan whose breed Ptolemy could not place, whickering in a distant stall away from the rest. "I hope the two of you are very happy."

Ptolemy laughed.

"What?" asked Sarah, as if suddenly unsure. "That's a normal thing to say.

"Ms. Lockhart," Johnson said, lifting a slender palm to gesture at a big, black German draft horse in a nearby stall. "This here is Callie." With those long, thick-knuckled fingers, he stroked the horse's nose. Callie leaned in, her wet brown eyes closing against his soothing touch. Then, she chuffed, letting out a long sigh. "She's been my best friend for years. Haven't you, sweet lady."

"About that mare," said Ptolemy, politely interrupting.

"Yes," said Johnson, patting Callie's nose once more and then moving up the row. "Now, her color will betray her to the naked eye as a palomino—until you see that Appaloosa snow-cap. And she's a big girl, especially for her breed. But that's what makes her perfect for you." He turned back to lightly backhand Ptolemy on the chest. "She'll carry your weight without a care in the world. And she likes apples, hates being penned in for too long. Too much of either and her weight will get away from you, and you don't want that."

Ptolemy shook his head. "I know how to care for a horse, J.J."

Johnson whirled on him, his cold, gray eyes gazing down at him in judgment. "You run this girl like you did that beautiful gelding, get her shot, well then you might as well shoot yourself, Gilbert, because I'll come for your hide like the devil himself. You hear that?"

Ptolemy bowed up and gave the grim man a measure of his own disapproval. "We were ambushed."

"I heard. And I don't mean to be so sour about it. He was just such a fine—"

"I know," said Ptolemy, each word chipped with ice. "He was my horse."

The stableman's lanky shoulders rose, and then relaxed entirely. "Right." He nodded, as if forgiving himself for the outburst and Ptolemy for the ambush. "Well, let me introduce you. She don't like everybody, but if she shines to you, she's sweet as they come." He walked past a few empty stalls to the tall mare.

Shafts of afternoon sunlight slanted in through the open windows, casting a champagne hue on her shining golden coat. Her mane and swishing docked tail were pale. The mare pricked attentive ears and moved toward the stall door to greet them. As she passed through a shaft of sunlight, it lit upon the snowcap of white blanketing her rear, from rump to thigh to hocks.

"Oh," said Sarah, stepping in front of Ptolemy. "Beautiful." Reaching out, she ran her dark fingers along the mare's nose. "Absolutely beautiful. What's her name?"

Jerry Johnson leaned an elbow against the stall, gazing at the mare. "Well, the name I gave her is one meant only for us."

Ptolemy reached up, enamored, and slid his hand along the mare's nose too. For a moment, and a moment too short, his fingers touched Sarah's. She let them linger half-a-heartbeat, maybe more, but not as long as Ptolemy wanted. He looked into the mare's eyes, scratched between her ears, then along her crest. "Only you would give a horse a secret name," he said to Johnson.

"Every horse has a secret name," said the stableman. "A first name. Then someone comes along and gives them a new one. The rider changes the horse, the same as the horse changes the rider."

"How romantic," said Sarah.

Ptolemy shook his head. "You didn't let me name my last horse. You just told me his name was Sunflower."

Johnson shrugged. "Things change, Gilbert. I have since become enlightened." He rolled his finger up to his brow, as if spooling a thread in the air.

Ptolemy smiled, then looked at the mare. "Sweet as you seem," said Ptolemy, considering for a moment, "I believe you're Vanilla, girl."

They rode out from the stable, leaving Jerry Johnson and thirty-five dollars behind, but bringing with them the golden horse, a brand-new saddle of brown supple leather and matching tack, and five apples red as the evening sun.

"She likes these," Johnson had said as he put them in the saddle bag. "Green apples, too. Don't let her go too long without one. She deserves it, good as she's always been to me. And besides, all beautiful women love sweets."

Sarah, to his surprise, had pulled herself up to sit behind him on the mare.

He'd only looked back, grinning.

"You don't think I'm gonna walk all the way back to my hotel, do you?"

She wrapped her arms around his waist, and for a little time they trotted through the streets of San Antonio, bouncing together in the mare's powerful gait.

Once Sarah had retrieved her own horse, Sisqo, they got out of the city. Ptolemy pointed them south and gave Vanilla a squeeze to see what she could really do.

The mare showed him. Over the trail of hard caliche well-worn by travel, Vanilla cut loose. She was so fast that even Sarah's quarter horse had to work hard to keep up. They passed by little farms and a small ranch along the wind-swept, three-mile journey to the mission. Ptolemy would have smiled the whole time were it not for the grave words of the Judge's telegram leaning hard on his mind.

About a half-mile out, the mission came into hazy view: first the stone belfry towers, a set of twins crowning what he guessed was the sanctuary, and then a single line of walls rowed in open archways. The mission was a welcome sight; however, its stillness—not one person working or walking around its grounds—was not.

He did not know much about the Catholic brand of faith, but he knew they took their worship seriously and had Mass at least three times a day. He hoped that was the reason for the lack of activity.

Ptolemy put up a hand and slowed his horse to a stop. Sarah rode up beside him, her gelding's loud breathing mingling with Vanilla's.

"Why are we stopping?"

"Listen," he said.

They were now a hundred yards, maybe less,

from the mission, but only the sound of the wind and the horses breathing filled the heavy air.

Sisqo let out a loud, shuddering chuff, as if displeased that his race with Vanilla was over. Sarah pulled his reins, drawing him back a step. "Easy, boy." Then she looked to Ptolemy. "What are we waiting for?"

"I don't like this," he said, scanning the mission, back and forth, along the north-facing edifice. The sun, a churning furnace, blasted the land so that there was only the heat and the light. The mission was baking in that sunlight. Along its well-worn perimeter all stood quiet, empty, still. Within the adobe walls of the mission's main body there was a fenced-in graveyard set before the sanctuary. Ptolemy could not count the depth of columns leading toward the church from this distance, but he could count the first row. And he didn't know why he counted them, but his eye caught them all. Fifteen crosses, running west to east, their gnarled weathering visible even from this distance. Short shadows leaned onto the ground, and the eerie quiet lorded over all. Sweat beaded along the back of his neck, running down his spine. "It's past midday," he said, keeping his eyes on the mission. "There should be people working in the field. Drawing water from the well. There are no mules, no horses either. Somewhere near twenty new folk just turned up here seeking sanctuary, but nary a one of them is outside?"

Sarah drew her revolver. "Yeah. I noticed all that too. So, again, Mr. Ptolemy, what are we waiting for?" There was a flat, emotionless quality to her voice—a sound Ptolemy had heard many times in his life, though from fewer people than one would expect. It was the sound of someone anticipating violence. The voice of a killer.

"Right," he said and gave Vanilla a kick.

They cut along the trail to the mission, the muted roar of the wind made from their riding spilled over thundering hooves, like two hearts beating wildly in the otherwise overwhelming quiet.

When they reached the walled-in graveyard, Ptolemy saw a bright red smear across one of the sanctuary's oaken doors. They dismounted and tied their horses to hitching rings set within the adobe walls. Ptolemy led the way with Sarah following close behind, both of them stepping beneath the timber arched entryway of the burial ground. Walking amid those weathered crosses, Ptolemy drew his pistol slow and easy and approached the looming, harrowed face of the church. With his free hand he pushed one of the massive iron-banded doors. It swung easily on its hinge, as if weighing nothing, opening unto the sanctuary.

The smell hit him first. The indefinable, unmistakable reek of death.

Next, the sight.

"I—" was the only word Sarah managed to say.

There were thirty of them at least, all sitting in the pews facing the altar. Some leaned to one side, as if dozing off during a sermon gone too long. Others, though they were upright, had their heads slumped, bowing as if frozen in reverent prayer. All of them quiet, all of them unmoving, facing the altar where six naked men sat bloody and bound. Ptolemy guessed them to be the mission priests. All six, set before the audience of the dead, had been disemboweled, flesh riven and pulled wide. Their intestines had been drawn from their flesh, unspooled and used to lash the men to the stone communion table of their god. Above the disemboweled corpses was a painting of Jesus Christ standing atop the crescent moon, illuminated, hands supplicant, glorified.

The stench of putrefaction and blood, waste and death was so powerful that Ptolemy feared he would retch..

Sarah passed by him, moving deeper inside, unflinching.

She walked down the aisle slowly, looking left and right to gaze upon the sitting dead.

Ptolemy looked too, sweeping the human

wreckage. Each had been shot once through the forehead, but there were no bullet casings, no damage to the polished wood pews or the adobe walls. Whatever had been done to these people, it had not been done in this place. And among the motionless dead, the eyes of a man captured the whole of Ptolemy's vision. Within their stillness was utter hopelessness, exhaustion residing in their vacancy. He gently took that man by the shoulder and leaned the body against the shoulder of the pew, shoulder to shoulder, as if to ease the man's burden, though that burden had already been laid down. There was dust all along the man's back. The base of his skull was caked wet and red, his hair hiding the wound that had ended him.

Ptolemy began to move on but stopped, arrested by the sight in the next pew. Another man, shot in the same fashion, but across his legs lay the body of a child, unweathered hands dangling limp. Small, smooth-faced, eyes closed. A little boy who would never run or laugh or play again. Who would never fall in love for the first time, never love again at all. Those who had taken this action against these people had taken more than this boy's life; they had taken all the living he had done before and all the living that could have been. All of the memories inside the father and his child annihilated, and their destruction was the desolation of all the love they would have birthed into the world. All the love that makes a man into a father. The love that grows the child into the man. The love that makes the world worth living in.

Ptolemy turned away, his heart tied to a string as long as the railroad tracks leading to Abilene. He missed his own boy—worried if he was alright. And then, incongruous to his worry, was a strange kind of relief; he thanked God that Carson had not come along with him, that his son was far away from this sanctuary which revealed none of God's hope and all of man's true nature.

Then there came a sound so loud it cut through his steely resolve. Not the sound of fear or terror or sorrow but the unmistakable bellow of rage. The sound of a woman who has lost and lost and lost and will no longer suffer a world that so easily takes. Sarah, one hand white-knuckled around her revolver grip and the other pressed flat against her face in furious anger, roared again. The afternoon sun slanting through the sanctuary doors shone upon her skin and the tears of wrath streaming down her face.

"Goddamn bastards!" she howled, looking up at the icon of Christ set before them, just beyond his mutilated servants.

Ptolemy stepped toward her and laid a hand

upon her shoulder. "There's nothing for us here. Come on."

Sarah did not give him her gaze, but only focused on the dead. "The law will do nothing for these people," she said, wiping her tears with the back of her hand. "You know that."

"I do," he said, squeezing her shoulder gently.

"We cannot let it stand, Gilbert." His name on her lips sent a shock of power through him, as if by naming him she had connected their furies. Intertwined their rage. And the heat pouring into that sanctuary from the sun outside was nothing compared to the wildfire in her eyes.

"No," said Ptolemy, knowing it was all there was to say. He slid his hand across her back, so that his arm mantled the woman in unspoken compact. "No. The Judge sent us here to hire these men. To give their families the lives they deserved."

"You know who did this," she said. "We both do."

Ptolemy nodded, considering Leslie Gramm's reputation for cruelty. "Yes."

They walked together out of that sanctuary, hip to hip, and by the time they passed under the timber arch of the graveyard gate, all the tears on Sarah's face had dried.

They headed north through a copse of cedar elms set afire in the reddening hue of the Texas dusk. Sarah asked Ptolemy to tell her everything the Judge had told him about Gramm. They were riding slowly, and Ptolemy was talking fast.

"Lieutenant Colonel Leslie Gramm owns a big section of land west of here. From what the Judge told me, it's a big ranching hacienda built and formerly upkept by those families in the church."

"How many men do you think he has?" asked Sarah.

"Don't know. But I figure if two armed Black folks come riding up to his property, we'll get a pretty good idea how many guns he's got."

Sarah swerved her gelding around an elm then back to ride close to Ptolemy. "We could sneak in under the cover of dark. Bar the doors shut. Burn them in their beds." Her voice was flat, matter-of-fact.

Ptolemy sighed. "That is not the way I do things."

Sarah looked Ptolemy hard in the face. "There's only two of us. Our only chance at making this right means using our single advantage of surprise. If Gramm has three guns or more, we're likely to lose. I don't have friends in this part of the world, Gilbert. I have no one to call on to help. It's just you and me."

Ptolemy looked among the elms, thinking hard. Among the trees came the cooing of mourning doves and the jays and purple martins japing one another. "Gramm may have family, children perhaps. They can't be blamed for what he did. His hands might have families too."

Sarah only stared at him, unmoved.

Ptolemy looked away, back up into the trees, considering. "Let's get a look at this hacienda, get an idea of what we're dealing with. But I'll tell you right now, Sarah, there ain't no way in hell I'm going to burn a man and his family alive."

"You'd rather get shot to pieces." For the first time since they had met, the woman leveled the sharpness of her tone against him. "Gramm ordered the massacre of those people. You know it. So do I. And I don't give a damn, Mr. Ptolemy, if your sensibilities get in the way of getting justice for this kind of barbarism."

Ptolemy nodded, though he did not agree. "How you dispense justice matters just as much as the justice itself."

She turned away, unhappy with him. "I like you," she said, "but that's some goddamn foolish talk."

"Then I am a fool."

"And frustrating," she said, the sharp slant of her tone easing. "But I'm not sure that I don't find it endearing, Mr. Ptolemy. Foolish and frustrating, but nevertheless endearing."

Ptolemy finally met her eyes. "I find you

endearing as well, Ms. Lockhart, and perhaps cold-blooded."

"I am as men like Gramm made me. I do not apologize for it."

Ptolemy could not argue with that, for he too had been crafted in the same cruel fashion by the cruel hands of men. "First light tomorrow, we'll have a look, then decide on our plan of action."

Sarah backed up her gelding, opening the way for Vanilla. "Sure, Gilbert. We'll have us a look."

They rode slowly toward San Antonio, letting the horses keep their strength. They'd asked a good deal from them in the rush to get to the mission, and they needed them fresh for another long ride tomorrow. Gilbert was glad to travel across that distance and length of time with Sarah Lockhart. He had never met a woman who was so quick to ask a question and quicker to tell you why your answer was wrong. Even when she considered his answers right, she still let him know how his position needed amending. She threw her inquiries at him fast and often. Ptolemy told her of how he had come into the Judge's service as a Peregrine Agent. And then he told her about Carson, whose biological father had purchased Ptolemy from a slave market before being driven mad by an occult tome. When the man tried to sacrifice his own son as part of a ritual, Ptolemy killed him to save the boy. "I took Carson as my own after that," he said as they rode under the swaying shadows of cedar elms, "and in doing so, saved myself."

"How do you figure?" Sarah asked.

"It is hard to describe," he said, bending his tall frame beneath an elm branch. "Even harder to explain."

Sarah laughed. "That doesn't get you off the hook. Try."

He shrugged, chuckling at how simply thinking about his son could draw tears to his eyes like a dipper draws water from a bucket. It was so sudden, the feeling, falling over him oh so quickly, and it was the only subject which compelled him in such a fashion. He looked at Sarah, opened his mouth, and then was forced to look away when his voice faltered. His and Carson's souls had been sewn together by the sharp needle of tragedy, and in the aftermath of the horror, they had chosen each other. No other subject pulled the threads of his heart so tightly, and he knew nothing else ever would.

"My, my, my," said Sarah when Ptolemy shied away. "Now if that isn't love on your face, I have never seen it before."

"I'm sorry," said Ptolemy, wiping the wetness from his eyes.

"Sorry for what?" She sounded almost angry.

"For not being able to answer your question," he said. "I want to. It's just that we've been through a lot together; I miss him very much, I worry about him while I'm here, and I think about what will happen to him if something happens to me. It's an odd sensation." He met her gaze. "Giving yourself so completely to someone. Knowing that you will need them for the rest of your life and the great weight of knowing they need you just as much."

Sarah regarded him kindly. "As a rule, I do not admire men, Mr. Ptolemy, but somehow you are proving an exception." And with that, she gave Sisqo a kick, setting him to a brisk trot. The wind caught her puffy hair as she rode forth, pushing through the copse of elms.

He watched her.

"She's something else, ain't she girl," he said, though Vanilla said nothing back.

The streets of San Antonio were dark save for the bars of light slanting yellow across the powdery dirt thoroughfare. Sitting within those lighted places, cooling themselves with whiskey and beer, were dusty cowboys and mule-skinners and desperate, hot-eyed gamblers burning over cards. Sarah and Ptolemy dismounted near a saloon named the Jolene Bean. Across the street there billowed a rush of guitar music and the rhythmic clapping of many joyous hands. Through one of the windows set near the saloon's doorway, Ptolemy saw a heavy-set Mexican woman dancing with the music, one hand clutching the trim of her skirt high above her head. Even from across the street and through the sheet glass, he could see that she was wild-eyed, pretty, sheened with sweat. She flowed across the saloon, passing from window to doorway to window, stamping her feet and spinning, possessed with the rolling flamenco music, the sharp crack of each clap and the heat of the night.

"Looks fun," said Sarah, coming around Sisqo to meet Ptolemy.

"Exhausting you mean." Ptolemy shook his head.

"You know those two things can coincide."

"I don't dance."

Sarah elbowed him gently in the ribs. "Who said I was talking about dancing, Mr. Ptolemy?"

He turned his head to look at her. "Well, I—"

She cut him off. "We should ask around about the ranch, see if anyone has an idea of how many guns this Gramm has on his property."

They went into the Jolene Bean and ordered a pair of whiskeys from the barman, who introduced himself as Oscar. He was a slender, curly-haired Mexican who brandished a butter-yellow smile below a thread-thin mustache. He flashed it often, jovial and quick to laugh at a customer's joke, no matter how bad it was. They drank at the bar, listening to the stream of sound through the saloon: the inconsequential gossip and threats and bawdy humor. Poker chips splashed pots of red and white and blue at the behest of gamblers, and empty shot glasses clapped tabletops at the urging of propositioning whores. And high above it all, reaching to the ceiling, was the hazy smoke of cigars and cigarettes and the pipe now in Ptolemy's mouth. After a while of asking and listening and gaining nothing in the way of helpful information from those around the bar, Ptolemy decided to level his inquiry at the barkeep.

"Wondering about the Gramm ranch," Ptolemy said, leaning in to talk to Oscar, straining to hear over the clamor. "What kind of outfit does he run? How many hands?"

The bartender's smile wavered, his eyes flicking down toward the end of the bar. Then, as quick as it had left, the smile returned. "Certainly, sir," he said, reaching below the bar to grab another bottle of whiskey. He poured Ptolemy another shot, though he'd not asked for one. Leaning close, Oscar said, "This saloon is often filled with Gramm's men, friend. They number five, sometimes six. All of them rough men who do Gramm's bidding, no matter what he asks. Come every two weeks when they draw their wages, spilling all their money and lust in a single night. They leave. Two weeks, they come back. My wife hates them. Cannot stand how loud they are. She also hates my saloon, the whores I employ, the whiskey I sell. She is a beautiful woman who despises my profession but loves the fine dresses it provides."

"When was the last time his men were here?" asked Ptolemy.

Oscar's smile widened, a knowing ken in his eye. "I think you are wondering more when they will next arrive, yes?"

"Yes."

"Two nights from now. And I know the line of these questions, friend. You are emancipated, free, and you have some vendetta against the old Confederate slaver, yes?"

Ptolemy shook his head and held his hat firmly on his head as he shot the whiskey. "I have no quarrel with him," he lied. Then, he told a portion of the truth: "I have never met him, but I know his reputation. I'm the proxy of a beef trader, Judge Hezekiah Ellison, in Abilene. He is wont to hire more hands, and we heard Gramm recently cut a swath of his loose upon Granger's Proclamation. Are any of Gramm's men here tonight?"

"Certainly, my friend," said Oscar, who then laughed at a joke Ptolemy had not told and leaned much closer than before, the distance of a shared secret. "The man down at the other end of the bar is Gramm's mercenary gun. A Silver Pin. Very dangerous, my friend. Arrived four months ago. If you talk with him, you will be careful, yes?" Oscar, still smiling, gripped Ptolemy's forearm. "If you have business with Gramm, promise me you will not see it through in the saloon my wife so desperately hates." He lifted his palms, gesturing at the patrons, the tables, the bar. All the things that so clearly meant everything to him.

"Oscar!" Sarah bellowed so loud that a table of gamblers all half-jumped out of their boots behind her. "Come pour me and my friend another drink," she bellowed, with one hand thrown over a drunken cowhand she was undoubtedly probing for information. The eruption of Sarah's voice was met with sharp silence, then low laughter among the crowd. And when the conversations began again they were quieter, a low hum now.

At that, Oscar feigned anger, slapping the bar top, then slid away toward the woman. He gestured wildly, hands flailing the air. "Yes, yes. Your whistle is dry," he said.

Ptolemy did not look down the bar at first, only into his drink. He stooped his head so that his eyes would be covered by the wide brim of his hat. Using his peripheral vision, he found the man in the space of recently emptied stools set between them, then slowly he lifted his head. The mercenary came into view a piece at a time: black boots, black pants, a fancy black crossdraw holster holding a nickel-plated revolver—too slender to be a .45 but heavy enough to make the holster sag. The sight had been filed off. A .38 most like. Set across the center of the gun belt was a long, smooth sheath holding a black horn-handled Bowie knife. Above the belt, a thick torso widened into a chest and shoulders and arms all jacketed in brawn. Weathered with age, the man's white skin was flush, dark pink, as if the Texas sun did not agree with his complexion. He was green-eyed with hair so pale it was almost as silver as the icon pinned to his lapel and etched with the number three.

The man was leaning forward, one foot set on the brass rail running the length of the bar, as if carrying the weight of the world on that silver head of his.

"I see you looking, mister," the man said, not turning to look at Ptolemy, "if you're thinking about getting famous, I promise you, taking a shot at me ain't the way to go." His voice was strange, nearly as high as a woman's.

Ptolemy shook his head, kept calm. "I see the pin, and I'm not looking for fame."

"Well, you're looking at me like I owe you something or like you're searching for something to take, and I don't much care for it."

"Word around here tells that you work for Gramm. You been with him long?"

"Why, you looking to buy my gun from him?" The man smirked, still gazing at the bar. "You don't look like you've got money. Nope, look more like a field hand to me."

Ptolemy let the insult pass over him. If Gramm had massacred those people at the church, then this gunfighter had probably been involved too. "No, I'm not the money, but I am here on business. I'm the proxy of a beef trader in Abilene—Judge Hezekiah Ellison. He asked me to come and speak with Gramm, get the state of the market, see if it was worth driving our cattle down this way or if we should keep expanding north."

The gunfighter snickered. "Well, you've come a long way for nothing. Gramm won't see you. See, he's got a particular disposition with shady folks such as yourself."

"How do you mean," Ptolemy said, the words dipping low in tone. It wasn't a question. It was a threat.

The man lifted his glass and took a series of long swallows until all the beer was gone. Then, he turned and appraised Ptolemy with those green eyes. Narrow, cold with malice, the eyes of a viper. "I've known the lieutenant colonel a long time and fought alongside him during the War of Lincoln's Aggression. He doesn't do business with you people. So, it's best if you run on back to your partner and tell him to take his fucking stock far away from San Antonio."

Ptolemy smirked, matching the man's unwavering gaze. "It's a real shame you say it that way. See, I'm real competitive, and damned if it doesn't make me want to bring our herd down this way and sell it for so cheap it sends you and Gramm to the poorhouse."

The gunfighter shrugged his shoulders. "I wouldn't let it come to that," he said. "I've got this real simple way of dealing with competitors." With that, he tapped the silver pin on his lapel. He lifted his high-pitched voice into the air and cut through the donnybrook of conversations spread throughout the saloon, silencing them all. "My name is Solomon Tate, and I am the Three within the Gunfighter's Guild. I've killed twenty-two pistoleers and countless others in war. Men and women of every living stripe. And still tickles me pink when I get a chance at killing a Black son of a bitch like you."

Tate's words carried. The room quieted. Still as a pond on a windless day, except for the coils of cigar smoke rising almost as high as the tension. Motionless seconds slid across time like a blade drawn across a whetstone, smooth, sharp, ready to cut.

"Interesting," said Ptolemy, unfazed. "Found myself a whole group of dead folks that look like me inside a Catholic mission, just outside of town. A massacre put on display. Reckon they were the folks who used to work for your boss.

You wouldn't happen to know anything 'bout that, would you?" He took a step toward Tate.

Most men would have tensed at his approach, but Tate's whole body seemed to relax.

Ptolemy was too far away to brawl, probably too slow on the draw to beat him outright in a gunfight, but he was close enough to see the truth in the man's eyes.

"No gunplay inside!" the owner called out from behind the bar. In one hand he held a mug, in the other the rag he'd been using to clean it, both hands raised high, emphatic. "This is my place, and no one is shooting any—"

It was the fastest draw Ptolemy had ever seen.

Solomon Tate's hand blurred and the sound of a single shot pierced the air. The mug shattered in Oscar's hand, and, before Ptolemy could react, Tate's revolver was pointed at him.

No, not at him. Just over his shoulder.

"You pull that piece, bitch, and I'll paint the bar with your blood."

Ptolemy had no doubt that Sarah had gone for her gun. After seeing the gunfighter's draw it was painfully clear neither Ptolemy or Sarah stood a chance. He shouldn't have approached Tate. Should have waited. Should have known better. And now, more than likely, he was going to get his head blown off in the middle of a saloon in San

Antonio. He thought of his son Carson. And when the boy's face came drifting up through the aching tension drawn taut between him and Tate, Ptolemy felt a great sense of negligence.

"Sir," said Ptolemy, attempting to somehow talk his way out of certain death.

"Shut the fuck up," said Tate, his voice breaking, sounding more like a pre-pubescent boy than a man shouting a command. "Now I'm issuing challenge. First to this beef trader who provoked me with insults, then to the woman he came in with. You all see this pin," he said, turning so that all in the saloon could see the pin on his lapel. "I am the Three within the Gunfighter's Guild, and my name is—"

"Solmon Tate," said a voice from the open doorway of the saloon, drawing the name out slow as a funeral song.

There was a shuffling sound of patrons turning in their seats to discover the voice's origin.

Ptolemy slashed his eyes over to the doorway to find his acquaintance from the train standing there leaning against the frame post, white-sleeved arms crossed over the red of his brocade vest. Oliver Maine's hat obscured his eyes and none of his grin. "I see you have met my friend Mr. Ptolemy. I say, let bygones be bygones, Mr. Tate." He lifted his chin so that all could see the clear intent living within his eyes. He smiled wide and gave Ptolemy a wink.

"And who the fuck are you?" asked Tate, incensed at the interruption.

"My name is Oliver Maine. I've come by way of a long road of killing, searching for you." He brought himself up to his full height, those hazel eyes looking cool and untroubled. He thumbed aside his vest, revealing the silver pin attached to his suspenders. "These people do not know you, Tate, but I do. Your true exploits. Your deeds. Tonight, all three come to an end. Within the rules of our association, I approach as the Four and challenge you, the Three, to a contest of the gun."

The room was still for about half a second, before one dusty, sunburnt farmer leaped from his chair, sending it toppling, and hollered "Ah sheeit" as he made a run for the door. He ran right past Maine and out into the moonlight.

No one else moved.

Maine rocked back on heels with that little laugh of his and turned to watch the farmer. When he turned back, he looked at Tate. "What'll it be Three? Accept or yield. I would advise the latter over the former."

Tate's face reddened. Sweat had formed on the man's brow, boiling hot as a potbelly stove. "Under the rules of our association, I accept your challenge. Name your time, gunfighter, and I will name the location."

"Well, I suppose the time depends on if you plan to test Mr. Ptolemy," said Maine. "I have grown fond of him and would hate to see him dead."

Sarah slapped the bar with one hand and hooted with laughter, drunk as a skunk. "Yeah," she said, lifting a shot glass with a slanted smirk on her face. "He'd have shot us dead." She tilted her head back and drained the glass in one swallow.

"This woman your friend, too?" Tate asked.

Maine shook his head. "I am sorry to say that she and I are not friends, because she is very beautiful, and I hate to see beautiful things come to an end. So, I do not believe I'll let you kill either her or Mr. Ptolemy. As the Four, I concede my right to name the time and grant it to you, under the agreement that you will forgo your challenge to these two until you and I have had a chance to settle our contest."

Tate's frown stretched to a sneer. He holstered his pistol and turned his mean gaze to Ptolemy. "Lucky you, shithead." Then the gunfighter twisted his brooding appraisal toward Maine again. "Tomorrow. Gramm Ranch. After lunch but before dinner time. Bring your own coffin if your hope is to be buried proper, else it'll be the buzzards for ya." With that, he stepped away from the bar and approached Maine. "Feel free to bring them along so I don't have to go find them when I'm done with you."

The two men locked gazes, nose to nose, and for a moment Ptolemy thought maybe, just maybe, they'd have it out right there in the doorway.

Tate bore down on the smaller man with a killer's stare.

Maine smiled the whole time, looking fearless of Tate, tomorrow, or the prospect of death.

Then Tate stepped past him out the door and into the hot San Antonio night. Slowly, the gambling and whoring and drinking and gossiping returned. Maine took off his hat and walked over to where Sarah sat slumped and misty-eyed at the bar. Ptolemy went back to his own drink, slugged it, then walked over to them, catching a conversation that had already begun.

"He was *very* fast," said Sarah, her words slurred.

"Yes," said Maine. "Very fast, Ms. Lockhart."

Sarah's eyes, heavy and red with drink, widened when she saw Ptolemy. "There he is. The tall, handsome man who nearly got me killed."

"Hell, woman, I didn't tell you to go for your gun," he said, frustrated. "Why would you go and do a stupid thing like trying to draw down on a member of the Gunfighter's Guild?"

"You put us in that situation by flapping your gums. Oh," she said. "*You are welcome.* I was happy to try to help you, and I accept your apology for being short with me."

Maine laughed. "Sharp as an Arkansas toothpick. I like you."

Sarah slanted that slice of moonlight smile toward Maine. "I do not admire men."

"How much have you had to drink?" asked Ptolemy.

Sarah narrowed her eyes, accusing. "You are a very angry, judgmental man, Gilbert Ptolemy."

"And you are drunk off your ass," he replied, then turned to Maine. "And you. . ." He extended his hand to the gunfighter. "You probably just saved my life."

They shook. "Maybe I did," said Maine. "Or maybe he would have missed. Perhaps you are the second-fastest gun in the world, my friend, and you would have killed him where he stood."

Ptolemy shook his head. "I have high confidence in my draw, Mr. Maine, but I am not delusional. No, I let my anger get the best of me. I saw his speed. He'd have won, no doubt in that."

"Perhaps. In any case, it wasn't luck that I walked in when I did." Maine reached over and snatched the full shot glass of whiskey Sarah was about to down.

"Hey!" she barked.

"Thank you, sweetheart. Saving lives is

thirsty business." He drank the whiskey, then handed the empty glass back to sulking Sarah Lockhart. "Checked around town. Folks told me Tate frequents this place, so I sat across the street—waited and watched him through the window for a while. It was tough giving him my full attention. They have this marvelous woman who dances, and my goodness if she doesn't steal the eye."

"So, you saw us come in," said Ptolemy.

"Sure did. Saw you engage with Tate too. And taking a little risk, waited a little longer."

"And by waiting—"

"I got to see how fast Tate is."

"And?"

Maine traced his fingers along his mustache with two fingers. "It's a hell of a thing, watching a person do what you do, only not as good. He's got a tell, a little hitch before he goes to pull. Costs him time. I'll snatch the life out of him tomorrow. Guaranteed."

"Good," said Sarah as she set her now empty glass on the bar and tried to stand up. She swayed, then steadied herself by taking Ptolemy by the arm. "After that, you can help us kill the rest of Gramm and his men." Then, she let out a long, cavernous belch.

Maine laughed. "Now, why in the hell would I—"

"Let's get a room," said Ptolemy, cutting off

the conversation. If they were going to have this talk, he didn't want to have it where so many ears could hear.

They rented one of the saloon's rooms from Oscar. He made them pay triple the room's normal rate because they had caused trouble in his place and would not be employing one of his girls to stay the night with them. Ptolemy paid, and they made their way inside.

The simple room featured a crude chest of drawers opposite a small woodstove, two oil lamps, and nightstands set on either side of its single extravagance: a plump feather mattress resting on an oak bedframe. A red bedspread covered the mattress and a pair of pillows. When Sarah sat upon the bed, her mouth fell open, forming a big O of surprise.

"It's so soft," she said. "Sure as shit softer than the one in the fleabag where I'm holed up." Spreading her hands along the bedspread, she looked up at Ptolemy. "Well, tell 'im."

Ptolemy leaned his weight against the wall, took off his hat, and rubbed his eyes. He felt the fatigue from the day now sinking marrow deep. Telling the whole sum of the story would drive that weariness straight past his heart, down into his soul. But he told it all the same, of what they had found at the mission.

"Each one killed with a single shot through the head, then taken inside the sanctuary and set upright. None were spared. Not even the children." Ptolemy gritted his teeth. It took him a few breaths to uncoil the anger writhing inside him, but he did. "The priests were mutilated, gutted, and strapped to the altar by their own entrails."

Maine said nothing, but his cool demeanor compressed, flattened hard as a sheet of ice.

Sarah, head down, smoothed the bedspread over and over.

"We believe Gramm sent his men to the mission to have them all executed. He is a known hater of our people," said Ptolemy. "Former slaveholder and Confederate. My guess is that when he had to let them loose, he couldn't stand it. Had them killed."

Maine shook his head. "Gramm may have given the order, but it was sure as hell Solomon Tate that did the killing. Of that I am certain."

"How?" asked Sarah.

Maine looked at her with those hazel eyes. And for a moment, Ptolemy did not like the intensity there, the primal magnetism. The way Sarah gazed back with sincere interest made him feel not afraid but somehow jealous.

"I learn about a person before I go after them. It's one of the ways a gunfighter stays alive: watching and listening and examining," said Maine. "During the war, Tate fought for the slavers as a hired gun in Mississippi. And in learning about him, I found out that one of the things he liked to do was to have his men pin a man down on his back, in the dirt, then he'd place his pistol right here." He placed his index finger between his eyes. "Fella I listened to said Tate loved it. Loved to talk to them, let them squirm and cuss and damn him, right before their rage ran out. When their courage left them and they began to plead for their lives, then, *bang*." Maine jerked his finger away from his head to mimic the gun's recoil. "They'd haul the body off, bring 'im the next one."

"Goddamn him," said Sarah, her eyes welling. "Goddamn them all."

"Yes, ma'am." Maine nodded his head quietly for a moment, thinking. "They were your people, and I swear I'll kill Solomon Tate for you. Tomorrow."

Ptolemy said, "A moment." He reached into his breast pocket and produced his pipe. Packed and lit it. Let the cool smoke fill his lungs. He nodded, considering all that he knew and all that was set before him. He thought about his son. The boy who comprised the whole shape of Ptolemy's love. And he thought about his oaths to the child. Felt the ache of looking into his grass-green eyes, the color of joy itself. Then, over that steadfast shape inside him, came pouring the memories of all the sons and daughters, husbands and wives, who had been whipped and slashed and burned and shot at the hands of men like Gramm.

Ptolemy blew out a long, blue-gray stream of smoke. "Tate isn't enough."

Sarah nodded. "Not even close."

"You want to kill all of Gramm's men," said the gunfighter." That goes beyond the scope of the challenge I issued, I'm afraid."

Ptolemy could hear in Maine's voice that he understood their meaning but could never comprehend the rawness of their reason.

"We *will* kill them all. Sure as blood dries black," said Sarah, mean and vengeful, not a single word slurred. Her anger had sobered her. He saw in her eyes a rage that burned hot as the fires of hell—and that was where she wanted to send them, Ptolemy knew, for they were siblings of the same rage; Sarah Lockhart just didn't give a shit who saw it. He could see it as clearly in Sarah as he saw it in himself.

Maine took in a deep breath, disappointment on his face. "As a member of the Gunfighter's Guild, unless I am employed by a patron, I can only challenge Tate within the rules of our association. I cannot help you kill a whole ranch-worth of gunhands. He could challenge you because you represented a threat to his patron's ends. You and I share no such affiliation."

Ptolemy shook his head, sucked his pipe. Blew out the smoke. The price of a guildhand, he knew, was beyond his means. He considered then how he might convince the man, perhaps by appealing to valor or justice. Explain that they were greater reasons than any guild rule.

But before Ptolemy could reason out the argument, Maine walked the length of the room toward him. "So, what do you say, boss? Five dollars to hire the fastest gun in the world?"

Relief washed over Ptolemy, and yet, without knowing why, he hesitated. "You're sure?"

The gunfighter's smile tumbled in a rockslide of seriousness. "Mr. Ptolemy, nothing would give me greater pleasure than to kill the men of my color who have done so great a calamity to the people of yours."

"What a deal," said Sarah three times in quick repetition.

Maine slipped his black felt hat back atop his head and ran his index finger along the brim. "It's late, and our business is concluded for the evening. I will retire. Ms. Lockhart, if you would permit me, I would gladly escort you back to your hotel."

Ptolemy smoked, implacable, refusing to show either of them how much he hated that idea.

"Why Mr. Maine," said Sarah, shooting him a sultry but surprised look, "I am quite capable of escorting my own goddamn self to my own goddamn hotel, thank you so goddamn much. But you are sweet to offer, I will grant you."

Maine sniffed a laugh.

Ptolemy grinned, smoke curling around his relief.

"Well," said the gunfighter, tipping his hat. "Then I shall leave the two of you. Mr. Ptolemy, I'll call upon you here in the morning. Have ourselves a little breakfast before our war." He nodded at Ptolemy, then at Sarah. "And good-night to you, Ms. Lockhart."

The gunfighter made his exit, that fearless smile ever on his face.

Sarah stood up from the bed and made her way to the door too. "It is late," she said.

Ptolemy was sorry to see her go. Despite all of the horror and blood and rage that had filled their time, there had been moments of genuine closeness between them. He wasn't ready for the day they had built together to crumble at the onset of night. "Well," he began, mimicking the smooth overconfidence of Maine's voice, "you don't have to leave. I could get another bottle? We could have ourselves a drink before 'our war.'"

Sarah stopped with her hand on the door but did not look back. "I've had enough whiskey for both of us already, Mr. Ptolemy," she said. There came a metal click.

He waited for the door to open, but it didn't.

"You know," she said, "ever since we were riding through that thicket back to town, I've been thinking about how this day would end." She turned and pressed her palms against the door. "Have you ever met someone who you were immediately drawn to, Gilbert? Like they've thrown an invisible lasso around your shoulders, and every time they talk it's like they're slowly pulling you closer without doing anything other than being themselves."

His heart quickened, which was quite the trick considering it felt heavy as a brick. He became immediately aware of the clamor filling the saloon outside and the aloneness the room provided them. He drew his pipe out of his mouth and, gazing hard at her, said, "Yes."

She tilted her head, letting her puffy hair shake like a blossom caught in a sighing wind. "That's how you make me feel. Most of me loves it, but a little part of me hates it. I know I say it, and it is true: I do not admire men. They've hurt me too deeply for me to give them the gift of my admiration."

"I am sorr—"

"Don't apologize for your kind. I wouldn't dream of apologizing for all the women that broke your heart or mistreated you. Just listen." She pushed away from the door and walked toward him, and her boots thumping on the hardwood floor become the only sound he could hear. That and her voice. "I know of you from Judge Ellison, and though the high praise one man gives another means little to me, he described your character as strong, seemed very admiring of you. Said I'd know you the moment I saw you. . ." She was only a foot away, her hazelnut eyes hot on him. "And you know what?" A single eyebrow lifted, and with it one side of her smile. "I did. I watched you get off that train, and I saw what kind of man you were in an instant. I followed you, wondering what your smile would be like, what your voice sounded like. And I wondered what you'd make of me." She stopped, inches away. So close he could have reached out and wrapped his big hands around her waist.

But he didn't. He waited. Listened.

"The moment you looked at me, I knew." She gently pressed an index finger into his shoulder. "You liked the way I looked."

"I do," was all he could say. It sounded dumb coming out of his mouth. Too matter-of-fact.

She reached up slowly, through the heavy silence between them, and took the pipe from his hand easy as plucking an apricot from a branch. Smiling, she turned the pipe around and put it in her mouth. She puffed the pipe, her eyes never leaving his.

Ptolemy, playing along, removed his hat and placed it on her head. The hat, much too big for the crown of her head, slid down, hiding her smooth brow.

"Perfect fit," she said, blowing the tobacco smoke toward him with her words. "Like it was made just for me." The tip of the hat tilted forward, slumping, covering those eyes, the smile, the pipe.

Ptolemy laughed, such a rare sound it surprised him.

Sarah set the pipe onto the little table beside them. With an upraised index finger, she pointed the brim high into the air, revealing the full beauty of her face once more. Then, with the same finger, she hooked the collar of his shirt and drew him forward. Their lips met.

The kiss changed the moment, the world. Changed the man.

Their hands found each other. His found her waist. Hers curled around his neck, a thumb tracing along his jaw. Though they were pressed into each other, in the imperceptible space between them roiled a maelstrom of passion. A power Ptolemy had never once known.

When he belted his arm around her waist and drew her close—so close that no matter after what happened after tonight, the circumstances of the world would never fit between them—that power seemed to flow through his fingertips, into her. She shuddered, kissed him harder. And they leaned into each other's strength. Undressed one another with fumbling hands.

Sarah, appraising him with her hands and wide, hungry eyes, took Ptolemy by the wrist and guided his hand between her thighs. She tilted her hips forward, pressing so that his reaching fingers slid deep inside her. And she sighed the sigh of an ache soothed, cinching his hand in place as she set her full weight upon his wrist. The heat of her breath against his ear, and the little words, conjuring a primal fire inside him.

Then, lifting off him, she took Gilbert by the hips and guided him to sit upon the bed. Never shying away from his gaze, never hurried, Sarah curled one arm around his neck, set her feet on the mattress, and curled her hand to grip the base of his manhood. Squeezing, she lowered herself onto him slowly. Her flesh was smooth to the touch. Her breath, drawn out in aching sighs, was hot, whiskey scented. The hunger in her eyes faltered for only the few seconds he witnessed a shudder roll through her. And, wrapping her strong hands around his neck, she stayed motionless for a time, pressing her breasts against his chest. Ptolemy felt their pounding hearts beating together. Then, their bodies found each other's rhythm. Up and down, never rushing, up and down, her throat set against his jaw. Fingers cupping his neck.

Sarah's motions became more insistent, as though she began to run ahead of him, chasing something. And as Ptolemy himself was reaching the culmination of his own pleasure, Sarah began to breathe hard, sucking wind through her teeth and blowing out harder. And harder. Faster and faster until, straining, she pressed the full heat and weight of herself upon him. There was a fluttering squeeze inside her, and that was too much for Ptolemy, and he felt a powerful rush roll through him like a hot, summer rainstorm.

Sarah leaned her stomach against his chest, still sitting atop him, and let out a little breath that became a giggle. The giggle became a laugh. The laugh that only earlier that day had changed him, changed him again. Sweaty, she slid away from him.

She turned, the lamp light catching her dark skin, turning it to bronze as she leaned down to gather her clothes.

"Where are you going?" was all he could think to ask, confused as he was. The stillness of the air, the quiet between them, expanded so rapidly that it shocked him.

Sarah slid a leg into her pants, then another, and pulled them up over her naked hips. "Back to my hotel," she said. "Where else?"

Standing there, shirtless and slashed across with the flickering light of the oil lamp and the waxing blue moon outside, Sarah Lockhart looked to Ptolemy like the most beautiful creation set upon the Earth. "Please," he said, much too softly. "Don't go."

"Stay? What, so you can listen to me snore off a drunk and I can wake up sweatier than I already am?" She slid her shirt over her shoulders, began buttoning it shut.

"Yes," he said.

Sarah's fingers slowed at a button, stopped.

He was not a man prone to desperation, but the idea of this woman leaving this place after such a moment swelled to life all the fearful distress within him. He had laid with only a few women in his life, and none of them had made him feel this way. None of them had seized him by the heart, set it on fire, and taught him the glory in letting it burn.

She gazed at him hard, her chest rising and falling, none of her playfulness in her eyes. There, in the hazelnut pools, Ptolemy saw both the pensive worry of prey and the hungry hope of the predator. The power of the woman. The ferocity.

Naked as the day he was born, he stood up from the bed and went to her. Of all the things he had wanted in his life, it was Sarah Lockhart he would forever want most. Her sharp mind and laughter, the fire of her eyes and. . . this. . . this connection. And not for just the here and now, but for the rest of his days. "Will you stay?"

Sarah shook her head. "I can't. . . have this. Even if we survive tomorrow, I have roads to travel. Scores to settle. And those places, Gilbert, are not the place to take a young boy. And the whole truth of it is this," she said. "I don't know this feeling. It's new to me."

"I feel it, too, Sarah," he said, finding the power in her eyes too strong for him to bear. He had stared down masters and killers and monsters, never cowing, but Sarah Lockhart—and the irrepressible strength resting inside her, the intensity that poured over him—proved too great a force to withstand. He counted himself fortunate to be the object of that strength. That desire.

Her slender fingers traced up his neck, delicately, each one trailing feather-light along his skin. Then she found the jut of his chin, cupped his jaw. The wind coming through the windows was cool, her touch warm on his skin.

"Perhaps," she said, the smile peeking out. "One day there will come a time when there are no scores to settle. No children to protect. If there is ever such a time, I believe I would enjoy spending it with you."

"There will be," he said. "Nothing good gets away." An old belief. One that pillared the firmament of his heart.

His words caught her off guard. He could see it in the way her lips pressed together. How her shoulders rocked back slightly, and her brown eyes widened, then wetted with tears.

The sound of the door-lock tumbling open broke the moment.

"This room is occupied," Ptolemy said before the door swung open and four men rushed inside.

Knowing their intent by the color of their skin and the menace in their eyes, Ptolemy turned to set himself between Sarah and the men, cocking his fists.

The first through the door, a freckled, red-headed man with a flat, pushed-in nose and a gap in his teeth wide as an open barn door, reached to grapple him. Fast as a rattlesnake strike, Ptolemy hit the man square in the fore-head and watched his eyes roll back and his legs turn to water. But before Ptolemy could swing again, one of the other men tangled with him, slithering into a clinch, and before he could turn and try to throw his attacker off, a second man kicked him so hard in the balls that the world went white. As he fell forward, a gunshot split the air, deafening him.

They have shot Sarah, he thought. They had come through the door and shot her—

Over the squealing whine in his ears, he heard the muffled sound of a woman's voice.

You should have gone for your gun, Gilbert, he thought, his groin pulsing with pain and nausea.

You stupid bastard. You should have gone for your gun. Now she's dead, and your son will be an orph—

"Fuckin' chicken-shit motherfucks," bellowed a raging Sarah Lockhart.

Get up. He tried to rally.

"Teddy!" a man screamed. "You shot Teddy!"

There was a scuffling sound.

"No," Sarah hollered.

Ptolemy set his hands on the ground, pushed hard, and tried to rise. To fight.

To win.

Then someone to his left kicked him in the face, and the world went black.

From a long way away, a grinding sound filled his ears. The distant churn of turning wagon wheels. He was jostled, bumping against the wagon's side. His hands were behind his back, tied so tightly that his fingers felt too thick for his skin. Lifting his eyelids a little, he gazed through his eyelashes to see the vague outline of a man sitting on the elevated jockey box at the back of the wagon. Though he couldn't make out much in the way of features, the figure was broad and masculine, with a rifle or shotgun set across his knees. The wagon rocked again, and Ptolemy used the motion to hide a slight downward shift of his head. He blinked hard, working to clear his vision. There, at the man's feet, lay Sarah, bound at the wrists and ankles, unmoving.

A strange kind of relief washed over him. They wouldn't have bothered with the ties if she was dead.

"Don't even think about moving." The words came from the man watching over him

Ptolemy kept his eyes shut, playing possum.

"You sons of bitches should have killed me when you had the chance," said another voice from behind him, near the front of the wagon. Ptolemy recognized it as belonging to Oliver Maine. All the relief he'd felt at knowing Sarah was alive washed out of him at the realization that they had captured Maine too. Probably ambushed him on the way to his hotel.

"Big talk, gunfighter."

"Just you wait," Maine said, his voice cold, confident. "You can't kill me, and you damn well know it. So does Tate. He and I are bound by a solemn oath, and when I get done with him, the rest of you will be next, you goddamn buffaloing cowards."

The man laughed. "Keep talkin', for all the good it'll do you."

Maine did not respond again.

The wagon rolled on.

Sarah stirred, cussed.

The man shoved her head with the heel of his

boot. "You keep quiet though," he said. "Quiet and real still, bitch."

Ptolemy lifted his head, ceasing to play possum, and took in the whole interior of the wagon. Next to Sarah, covered in a bloody riding blanket, lay a body—presumably the man she had shot. The man sitting on the jockey box was dark blond, ruddy faced. The red dawn slanted across his brow, catching the blue of his eyes and the sandy color of his beard. He gripped the shotgun across his knees, adjusting with the jostling wagon. "You too, big fella," he said.

"Who are you?" asked Ptolemy.

"Name's Jack Silverton," he said, simply.

"And you work for Gramm, no doubt," said Maine.

"I do."

"Guessing this wagon is taking us to that estate of his," said Ptolemy.

"Got it all figured out, don't ya, big fella," said Silverton. "Sure is. We're taking you up there, all of ya." The man looked to Maine. "You, gunfighter, we'll give to Tate. You other two. . . well, let's just say Mr. Gramm would like to meet the proxy of this cattleman from Abilene."

"I'd like to meet him too," Ptolemy said, putting a clear threat in his words. "Ask him about what we found at that mission."

Silverton gave a malicious grin. "Why, sir. I haven't the slightest idea what you mean."

Ptolemy stared at the man, burning with rage.

The wagon passed through an iron archway set between two long stretches of a low rock-and-mortar wall. Looking out of the back of the wagon, Ptolemy saw several men move from their posts at the fence, each of them carrying rifles, approach.

One of them, a tall, gangly man wearing dusty brown threads and a straw hat spoke first. "Well, looky look at what Jack's brought back," he said in a heavy Irish accent.

"Hey, Jack," another man called out from somewhere Ptolemy could not see, "is Teddy with you?"

Silverton shook his head, swung his legs over the side of the wagon, and dropped down. "He is, Bobby, but I'm afraid he can no longer be counted among the living."

"Well, hellfire." A short and spindly man came into view around the back of the wagon. His tan face was cracked worse than a saddle abused by too many rides and too many years in the desert sun. "I liked Teddy." He pushed his black, stringy hair out of his eyes. "You figure Gramm will let me have his roan?"

Silverton laughed. "Christ, Bobby. His body ain't even cold yet."

"You're right." He nodded, considering, with pouted lips. "I can wait till we've put him in the ground. But you heard me call first claim on the roan." He turned and looked into the wagon, crossing his arms across the jockey box. "Morning."

"Go fuck yourself," said Sarah.

The man laughed, gave Ptolemy an appraising eye, and then turned his attention to Maine. He pointed. "You must be Oliver Maine. Heard of that famous right hand of yours. I'm Robert Gary. Folks call me Bobby though."

"Pleasure's all yours, Robert," said Maine. "Now, untie me and get me out of this wagon. I've got business with Tate."

A happy cruelty stretched across the man's cracked face. "Tate's at breakfast with the lieutenant colonel. Told me to take you to meet Creek before the two of you settle your affairs. So, come on, gunhand. Nice and easy like."

"And us?" asked Ptolemy.

"You two have other business," said Silverton, dropping the gate of the wagon bed. "Come on out here with me, honey." He snatched Sarah by her hair and dragged her roughly over the lip of the wagon bed, where she fell out of Ptolemy's sight.

Gramm's gunhands were all given over to whooping laughter, slapping their legs and bending at the waist, blanketed with glee at the power they lorded over the bound.

Ptolemy went to rise, tear free of the ropes and fill his hands with their throats, all of them, each and every one, and squeeze, silence all their laughter until their irises expanded, freezing as the shroud of death covered their eyes forever.

Silverton caught Ptolemy's glare. "Oh, boys, look at what we have here."

Bobby and the Irishman joined him to peer in at Ptolemy, the three of them all lean, narrow-eyed, grinning like a den of foxes.

"Looks like he'd rather fight than have breakfast," said Bobby.

"Looks that way, don't it, Jack," said the Irishman.

Silverton's vulpine grin fell away. "No reason he can't have both."

"Gilbert," said Maine, the preamble of a warning. But it was too late.

All three men scurried up into the wagon bed and, as a collective body, took Ptolemy by the shoulders and flung him, sweaty and still naked, over the jockey box. Ptolemy, with his arms tied behind his back, hit the hard ground face-first. The world flashed. Something gave way in his shoulder.

He damned the pain and rose to his knees, bringing all his strength to twist and pull against the ropes binding his hands. He stood, turned to face the three men now stepping off the wagon bed. He'd known the bite of such ropes before in his life, learned from those moments, and pushing the knuckle of his thumb hard, he used his sweat and muscle to wriggle his hands free.

"Aye, god is he persistent," said Bobby, approaching without fear, without going for the pistol tucked in his belt. Running his fucking mouth. "Braver than I'd be with my pecker hangin' out in the—"

Ptolemy looped all his strength into a single punch that caught Bobby just below the cheek. The man's leathery, cracked face twisted, his eyes shut, and he fell. Ptolemy snatched up the pistol from Bobby's belt, brought it up, and aimed the barrel sights at Jack Silverton, who stood pointing his shotgun at Sarah's back.

"Easy," said Silverton.

The Irishman in the wagon had drawn his pistol and rested it on Maine's shoulder.

"Bobby," said Silverton, "you are one dumb son of a bitch."

Bobby, chin in the dirt, ass up in the air, was snoring. Unconscious.

"You've got a set of balls on you," said Silverton to Ptolemy.

The Irishman laughed. "Clearly."

Silverton shoved Sarah's motionless body in the back with the killing end of his shotgun. "Three. . ."

Ptolemy grit his teeth, considering if he was fast enough to—

"Two…"

He tossed the pistol into the high brush, just beyond the rocky wall.

"Good," said Silverton. "Good boy." Keeping his eyes on Ptolemy, he cocked his head toward a row of bunk houses with adobe walls. "Wally, take Mr. Maine over to visit with Creek. Then fetch some clothes for our naked friend here. He looks about Teddy's size."

Sarah groaned, rising once again to consciousness.

"Shh now, honey," said Silverton, putting his heel into her back, pinning her down. "Everyone just take a breath and relax. Hell, you all ain't even had your breakfast yet."

The Irishman escorted Maine away and into one of the small buildings just north of the bunk houses. Gray smoke roiled out its soot-blackened chimney stack. The door shut behind them, and for a short time they all waited, Sarah still pinned down, Ptolemy staring at Silverton.

Silverton produced a flask from his vest and took a swig from it.

Bobby stopped snoring and began to moan, his hands reaching up to cradle his jaw. He tried to say something. Then, his eyes widened in stark realization. And with indeterminable words from that ruined mouth of his, he uttered a maligned protest.

"Well, Bobby, looks like our man here did everyone a big goddamn favor and busted that jaw of yours."

Bobby, forgetting his injury, shot a hand to his belt and groped for the pistol that was not there. He looked up at Ptolemy, the epiphany in his eyes flaring to rage. Balling his fists, he scrambled to his feet, ready to fight once again.

"You've got sand," said Ptolemy. "I'll give you that."

"Bobby," said Silverton, apparently foreseeing what the man was about to do. "Don't!"

Ptolemy saw it too: the desperate swell of a man who has taken much too long to act and thus commits the unpardonable sin of the scared art of the brawl—hesitation. Bobby drew his hand back to lob a haymaker, and Ptolemy snapped a straight left hand into his weathered face. Bobby's nose bent from the impact, shattered, and blood exploded from his nostrils. His eyes rolled back, white. Arms stiff as a wooden post, he fell to the ground.

"Jesus Christ, *Bobby*." Silverton leveled the shotgun at Ptolemy. "Alright, alright, that's enough."

The Irishman emerged from the bunk houses alone, carrying a bundle of clothes and a pair of boots. He sauntered over, looking over Bobby then back to Ptolemy, menace in his smile. "Hell fire," he said, handing the clothes to Ptolemy. "You hit 'im again? Mr. Gramm ain't gonna take kindly to that. And you already got it bad enough already."

As Ptolemy dressed, Silverton pulled Sarah to her feet, whereupon she swayed back and forth for a moment, unsteady.

"Good god," said Silverton, turning up his nose. "You smell like shit."

She spit in his face.

His eyes flared in surprise, then he slapped her hard for her trouble. The impact gave a dull, flat sound. Sarah staggered backward but kept her feet.

She grinned a bloody grin at Silverton and lifted her chin. "That all? Or do you need another try?"

The rage in his face melted, and he laughed. "Aye, god, are you full of sass." He swung the shotgun, cradling it at his hip so that it pointed at her belly. "I suggest you keep that smartass mouth of your shut. Unless you think you're bulletproof."

Sarah's smile did not diminish, though she said nothing.

"Maine?" Silverton asked the Irishman.

"Should've seen the look on Creek's face," Wally said. "He's gonna have some fun with that one."

The two men ushered Ptolemy and Sarah at gunpoint up toward the grand adobe hacienda and then along a narrow path that led around the back. The many dark windows they passed revealed nothing of the hacienda's interior. The path led to a large cedarwood pavilion where two men sat at a fine table covered in bright red, blue, and yellow Talavera tiles.

One man was Solomon Tate, leaning back in his chair, his green eyes peering at the newcomers over a fine china coffee cup. The other, sitting at the head of the table with a languid elbow resting on the back of his chair, was a bald, grim-looking man with a silver handlebar mustache. He was mantled in a burgundy frock coat, and his eyes were bright blue sapphires in the morning sun. Before them, the table was covered in golden platters, cups, and plates, gleaming in the light.

"Finally," said the bald man, his voice happy, carefree. He leaned forward, took a quick sip of coffee while halfway to standing, and gave a flourish with his free hand. "Please, please. Come sit."

Gilbert and Sarah, still at gunpoint, were seated next to each other, opposite of Tate.

"As you might have guessed, I am Leslie Gramm. Formerly a Confederate lieutenant colonel, but now just a lowly cattleman." He extended his arms, palms raised, and sat back down. "Mr. Tate here tells me your name is Gilbert Ptolemy, and that you represent the interest of a competing cattle company near Abilene. A mister. . . what was his name?"

Ptolemy stared at the man. "Where have you taken our friend?"

"Impetuous," said Gramm. "There's no grace or formality to you at all, is there." He sniffed a little laugh.

From a distance, over the silence between the captives and captors, there came a harrowing sound muted by thick adobe walls, a scream that rolled over the landscape, clawing its way into Ptolemy's ears.

"Ah," said Tate. "Oliver Maine has become acquainted with Creek."

Gramm smiled and turned his attention back to Ptolemy. "His name? The principal for whom you proxy?"

"Judge Hezekiah Ellison," said Sarah. "We are both agents of his."

Gramm feigned surprise. "She speaks. Ellison, is it? I have never heard of him. Tell me, darlin', is he a wrathful man?"

"You mean, if you kill us, will he send others for revenge?" she asked.

"I mean, if I sent this Judge Ellison a pretty box with a nice little bow wrapped around it, with your head inside, would he understand that in seeking revenge with me, he would be testing Death itself?"

"Come and take it," said Sarah.

Gramm's smile soured, and his eyes narrowed. "In time, darlin'. In time."

"They're just upset," said Tate, checking his pocket watch as though he were bored.

"Yes," said Gramm. "With what you two found at the mission, well. . ." He shifted in his chair, clearly enamored with the sound of his own voice. "I am sure to see such a thing would be upsetting for those who do not understand the full purpose of the decision."

"So, you admit it," said Ptolemy.

Gramm shook his head, as if confused by the sharpness in Ptolemy's tone. "Freely. They were mine, to do with as I please. I bought them, fed them, put a roof over their heads. Gave them a purpose in the upkeep of my lands. And never, not once, did I discipline them out of cruelty. There is no cruelty in me. Of all the masters they might have known, I am certainly the most kind. The first among the best. And yet, by insisting on going their own way after all I did for them, they wounded me, you must understand. They cut me to the quick. The fever of abolition drove the stock mad, and there is only one thing a responsible cattleman can do when such a sickness invades his herd."

Ptolemy's teeth grit together so hard, Gramm heard it.

"See, even now, when I explain it to you in the plainest of terms, you grow angry. Your rage blinds you to reason, to logic. Just as I expected." He leaned forward as if to impart a secret virtue unto the quiet world. "There are moments when mercy must wear the robe of annihilation."

For all of the great capability within his hands, Ptolemy did not move. Though his heart stirred with a rage born of his own wounds and the collective wound born of an incalculable subjugation, he kept still. He knew that if he rose to kill Gramm, he'd never reach his goal; he'd seen Tate's quickdraw.

"I know," said Gramm, mistaking Ptolemy's patient inaction for revelatory awe. "These are all hard truths for you to hear. Though they are the truth all the same." His mustache lifted as his mouth curled up.

"Colonel," said Tate, "Reckon Maine will be ready now. I'm ready, too."

"Ah, yes," said Gramm, then took a final, hurried sip of coffee like a man running behind schedule. "Your guild affair comes first. Then we shall get to the business of sending our parcel to this Judge Ellison of Abilene."

"Yes, sir." Tate flashed his green eyes at Ptolemy. "If you have tears, prepare to shed them now."

Gramm and Tate left the table, leading the way back around the main house. Ptolemy and Sarah were made to follow at gunpoint. A mixture of dread and hope filled Ptolemy at that moment, for he saw in Tate's eyes the same confidence that Maine had so easily brandished. The sureness of self. The prophetic fires where victory is a foregone conclusion. He remembered all that Maine had said in the bar car of the trail-runner train, his harrowing tale of surviving death many times over. And he recalled how easily Maine had perceived Tate's tell. Remembered all Maine's boasts and all his claims. The fearlessness swirling inside the sunflower rings of those hazel eyes and the aching maelstrom churning beneath, so desperate to be set loose upon the world.

And all that confidence, all that surety of success, rose to the topmost height within Gilbert Ptolemy, so that even with a shotgun barrel not two feet from his spine he found himself smiling like the devil.

"Creek!" Tate bellowed as they came to the long stretch of powdery dirt road set between the hacienda and the adobe bunkhouses. The sun flared hot and bright, bleaching white the bald caliche thoroughfare.

"You may spectate from here," said Gramm, as he moved over to the side porch of his home.

He sat in one of three oak rocking chairs beneath a large window of colored glass.

"What if Maine wins? " asked Sarah Lockhart.

At this, Gramm crossed one leg over the other, laughed. Shook his head.

"They'll kill him in the street," said Ptolemy to Sarah.

"So that's it," said Sarah.

And it was there, for the first of what would only be two times in his life, that he heard Sarah's voice break. In the tragedy of its sound, he felt all the world's troubles and injustices. And to hear it from her, a woman of such remarkable grit and resilience, was to ache to hear it mended.

Ptolemy wanted to say something to her, truly. He wanted to tell her how sorry he was for not having taken the fiery revenge she had so desperately wanted to put upon these people in the middle of the night. Wanted to tell her he would protect her. Make all the promises he knew she would hate to hear. But before he could say any of these things, before he could will into the world the miracle that would supplant their captivity, Oliver Maine came into view. What the sound of Sarah's voice breaking had done to his heart, the sight of Maine did to his soul.

Hatless, he was shoved out of the dark doorway, where he tumbled into the dust. And the way he fell seemed unnatural. Though he tried to catch his weight, he spilled into a roll that landed him flat on his back. His face was as red as his brocade vest, the garment matted with blood, and his eyes swollen near shut.

"Oliver Maine," said Tate, mocking, drawing out the gunfighter's name slow, almost sarcastic. He sauntered toward him, taking his time, one hand resting on the butt of his revolver.

Maine coughed. A desperate, rasping sound.

"I am the Three," began Tate, a herald of destruction. "You, as the Four, have come unto me in opposition, to test my skill for the sake of my number and my pin. I approach you in honor, within the rules of our association, and hereby challenge you to a contest of the gun."

A shirtless man, slender and bent as a fishing hook, stepped out of the dark doorway behind Maine. With tan skin and long black hair, he cut a lean, dangerous shape against the prairie morning. He was wringing his red hands on a white cloth, further reddening the fabric with every twist. "Here," said the man who must be Creek. He set his hands beneath Maine's arms and hoisted him to his feet.

"Oh god," said Sarah, seeing before Ptolemy saw.

Bought up to a hunched height, Maine was turned so that the whole of the man could be seen. And what they had taken.

His right hand dangled free and loose below the French cuff of his fine, blood-stained shirt. Where the left hand should have been was a blackened stump jutting from a torn sleeve, also slathered with blood.

A sickness roiled in Ptolemy's stomach, knotted by ropes of revulsion and terror and rage.

Creek released Maine's shoulders and gave him a gentle shove toward Tate. Maine moaned, tipping into his opponent's arms.

"Ohh, Four," said Tate. "This was your moment! Look, look to your friends."

Maine groaned, unable to lift his head.

Tate snatched Maine by the chin, lifting his cowed, swollen eyes toward Ptolemy and Sarah. "I said look, goddamn you. You look!" Tate slapped Maine across the face lightly, then again. Even the little blows nearly knocked Maine to his knees. Tate, confident and mean, held Maine erect. "Since you are unable to meet the demand of our contest, I guess I will just have out my business with these two first." And he let Maine go and drew his pistol, twisted at the hip and fired. It was smooth. Fast. Accurate. The bullet slashed the air, singing through the small gap between Sarah and Ptolemy, where it slammed into the adobe wall of Gramm's home behind them. Jack Silverton, standing just behind Gilbert with that shotgun of his, gave a holler.

To her credit, Sarah hadn't so much as flinched.

The gunshot echoed. Tate waited for the sound to die before reloading his gun. "How's that, Four? Could have killed either one of them, and after we've settled our business, I'm going to—"

Maine mumbled something. A low sound.

Tate kept those killing eyes of his on Ptolemy, but they widened in happy surprise. "What's that, Four?"

Shivering with pain, hair darkened with sweat, Maine swayed, unsteady. His shoulders sagged, then rose as he took a deep breath. "Challenge accepted," he said.

Tate twisted suddenly, his heels grinding the little stones beneath his dust-powdered black boots. "What?"

Maine, diminished in all physical measure, lifted the stump of his left arm and slid its charred ruin between the glimmering golden buttons of his vest, transforming the garment into a sling. "My name is Oliver Maine. I am the Four. I accept your challenge, Three." The sun caught the sheen of sweat pouring off him, setting the white skin of his mangled face to shine like polished soapstone in the late morning light.

"You accept?" said Tate, uncomprehending.

Creek cackled. "Hell, Tate, he's still game. Maybe I should take that other hand, too, huh?"

Tate was scared of Maine—that was all too clear now—so scared that he'd gone and rigged the contest. Ptolemy didn't know a great deal about the Gunfighters Guild, but he was pretty goddamn sure that cutting off a person's draw hand was against the rules. And that thought triggered something in his mind, a memory of a comment Maine had made in the train. *"With my left hand I am the equal of every gunfighter in the world. With my right I am their superior."*

The hope inside Ptolemy dared to breach the surface of his heart once again.

Maybe, just maybe, Oliver Maine was everything he said he was. Everything he believed himself to be.

"What greater advantage do you need, Tate?" Gramm called from the porch, a little annoyance in his voice. "You've taken his gun hand. Let's get on with it and then get out of this disagreeable heat. Christ."

"Fine," bellowed Tate. "Where's his pistol?"

Creek reached behind his back and produced Maine's pistol from his belt.

"Give it to—" Tate began.

"No," said Gramm, shaking his head. "You gunfighters are as fast as you are careless. Creek, first remove all but one bullet from Mr. Maine's gun."

Ptolemy looked back at Silverton, still holding the shotgun, much too far away to rush.

"Nothin' back here for you, boy," said Silverton. A final warning.

Ptolemy's heart beat slowly, the slim hope he'd dared let rise came crashing down. Even if Maine was faster than Tate, one bullet was enough for conquest, too few for salvation.

"One bullet or all six," said Tate, his voice filled with venom. "It don't fucking matter. Let's get this over with."

Creek did as commanded, pocketing five shells, then sliding the revolver into Maine's blood-matted gunbelt. "Best of luck to ya." He cackled again as he shuffled back toward the safety of the bunkhouse.

Tate walked several paces away, counting each one until he came to twenty-five.

Maine, standing with his back to Tate, looked over at Ptolemy. And from within the shadows of his swollen, bruised face, his hazel eyes shone. He shot Ptolemy a smile—one that delivered all the charm and confidence of a man fearless of death.

Sarah reached out and took Ptolemy by the forearm.

"Good luck with that hand of yours, Mr. Maine," said Ptolemy.

Maine nodded, smile widening.

Ptolemy filled his mind with the face of his

son, knowing that he would never look into the eyes of that beautiful child ever again. Tears blurred his vision.

"For what it's worth," said Sarah, "I have come to admire you."

He looked at her, seeing all that was best. She had rendered him speechless

"Turn, coward," cried Tate, impatient. "Turn!"

Maine did not turn.

But he drew.

Until the end of his days, it would prove to be the fastest draw Ptolemy would ever see.

There was a bright flash, the pistol catching the sunlight, and a cut of wind between Sarah and Ptolemy. The whip crack of gunfire.

Ptolemy followed the wind, turning to see a dime-sized hole in Silverton's head between eyes that would never see again. The shotgun slipped from Silverton's fingers.

There was another gunshot, and Sarah screamed. Ptolemy lunged for Silverton's shotgun, grabbed it with one hand and snatched up the dead man's pistol with the other. And he and Sarah were moving fast to take cover behind the hacienda's corner.

Gunfire peppered the air, bullets spraying the ground and the adobe wall over their heads.

"Goddamn it!" Gramm yelled. "Goddamn it all!"

Crouching beside Ptolemy, Sarah took the shotgun from him. "Tate's empty," she said, her eyes widening.

He turned to look back to the street. Maine lay in the thoroughfare, unmoving. And not twenty feet from the body was Solomon Tate, reloading.

Tate might be one of the fastest gunslingers alive, but Ptolemy found himself to be the most patient. He stepped around the corner of the hacienda and breathing slow and steady, looked down the barrel at the gunfighter.

"Tate!" screamed Gramm from some unseen place, warning.

Tate had just enough time to look up before Ptolemy fired. The gun bucked. Tate twisted, howled.

Ptolemy kept walking forward, pulled the hammer back and fired again.

A tuft of Tate's shirt flapped, spraying the gunfighter's hair with his own blood.

From the bunkhouse door right next to them, Creek appeared, screaming a war cry and holding a bloody cleaver up high, ready to throw.

Ptolemy aimed at the howling maniac, fired again. The man's chest opened, blossoming scarlet.

"Ah, Christ," cried Gramm.

Ptolemy turned to see Gramm scramble from

behind the rocking chairs, making a break for the door to his palatial estate.

But Sarah came around the corner, shotgun raised.

Gramm froze, put his hands up.

Sarah approached until she was no more than five feet away.

Gramm began to plead. "No, no wai—"

She unloaded both goddamn barrels.

Gramm's terrified face became a wave of red, turning to mist.

Tate, groaning, tried to turn over, to bring himself up to fight once again.

Ptolemy kicked away the man's pistol.

"Goddamn you," cried Tate. "Goddamn you!"

Tugging the gunfighter by his bloody sleeve, Ptolemy flipped him over.

Tate's face had lost all its color, and there was no fight in those eyes, only impotent rage.

"You—" Tate began.

But he got real quiet when Ptolemy placed the barrel against his forehead. Just as Tate had done to so many others at the mission, and so many who had begged for mercy before that.

"I... I..." Tate stammered.

"Say he was faster."

"What?"

Ptolemy pulled the hammer back on the revolver, relishing each click. "Say he was faster than you."

Tate shook his head as if unable to comprehend.

"Say he was the fastest gunfighter in the world."

There came a shuffling of feet from behind him: Sarah approaching, perhaps to watch the killing.

Tate grit his bloody teeth, his lips peeled back in a snarl, incapable of repeating the truth.

"I assure you, Mr. Ptolemy," came Maine's weak voice, "I am the fastest."

A wash of relief poured over Ptolemy. He turned to see Maine being held upright by Sarah, the afternoon light throwing itself over them both, radiant.

"And the more accurate," said Sarah.

Ptolemy turned back to Tate, whose eyes were wide with rage.

"End it," said Sarah.

And with a squeeze of the trigger, Ptolemy did.

They made all haste helping Maine to the wagon. Sarah drove the horses out of the hacienda back toward town, and Ptolemy stayed in the back of the wagon with Maine, holding a rifle ready and scanning for any sign of Bobby or Wally or any damn other hand who had worked for Gramm.

But no one answered his final gunshot, no one gave chase.

Over the sound of the galloping horses, Sarah yelled back to them from the driver's seat that she was adding their names to her long list of scores to settle. She made a promise that after they got Maine to a doctor in San Antonio, she would make every effort to find those cowards.

They raced on through the afternoon heat, driven by the power of nameless horses under the persistent calls of Sarah Lockhart, until eventually San Antonio came into view. They found a doctor near the Main Street hotel, where they quickly carried Maine inside.

Sarah and Ptolemy were asked to wait at a little table in the front lobby, where they both sat bloody and exhausted.

And though Ptolemy had much he wanted to say to the woman sitting next to him, he could not bring himself to say it. Sarah also kept silent, spinning in her fingers the silver pin they had taken from Tate's body.

So, Gilbert Ptolemy said nothing.

And Sarah did not smile.

After the surgery to remove the bullet, the doctor, a raven-haired, bespectacled man by the name of Bolivar, had them help carry Maine to a spare bedroom. Then he tried to shoo Ptolemy and Sarah away so he could focus on his work. However, before they left, Sarah gently removed

Maine's silver pin etched with the "4" and replaced it with the one inscribed with a "3."

"Come back in a few hours," the doctor said. "I'll know more then." And he shut the bedroom door on them.

They walked out into the thoroughfare, where women visited grocers or shopped for dresses, some of them accompanied by doting men whose hair was slicked with pomade. A group of cowboys moved a little remuda past the Alamo, whooping and whistling, carefree and happy. The wind picked up along the busy streets, and the world went on, indifferent to all their peril.

"Tell Maine I was glad to meet him," said Sarah as she walked ahead of Ptolemy, striding toward the saloon where she had left Sisqo. "I'll wire Judge Ellison on my way out of town. Let him know. . . know what happened. He will want to know all of it."

He said her name.

She stopped, turned. There were tears in her eyes, but she did not let them fall. "I suppose you'll go back to your boy now, and I back to my life before you."

"Yes," he said, approaching.

"Good." She pressed her lips hard together and nodded. "He needs you. And I have no use for men."

"Sarah, I—"

"No," she said. "No, I do not believe I will let you say more." She wrapped her arms around his neck and kissed him with all the fire and passion they had known only the night before. A fire Ptolemy hoped he would one day feel again.

And she turned, went along the street through the whooping cowboys and their stalled remuda, along the crowded shops and their customers, where no one gave her much notice at all. And Gilbert Ptolemy watched her, each and every step, until she walked into the distance under the sun that they, for a single night, had touched together. Around the corner she went, never once looking back, as she walked out of his life.

Ptolemy went back to the saloon to gather his things from the room he'd shared with Sarah. He asked for a bottle of bourbon from Oscar, who all the while assured Ptolemy that he'd done everything he could to stop their abduction.

"I am just a saloon owner, my friend," he said, holding out the bottle of bourbon. "If I were to die, who would take care of all this?" He gave a professional smile. "I am glad to see you survived. Tell me, did the others make it out alive with you?"

Ptolemy took the bottle from the man, said nothing, and did not pay.

He returned to the doctor's office and waited

outside for hours, turning the bottle in his hands.

After much too long, Bolivar opened the door, looking exhausted. "Your friend is a strong one. And he is lucky. The bullet passed through him clean. And cauterizing the arm saved his life."

"So, he'll live?" asked Ptolemy.

The doctor grinned, "Death passes by this office with great frequency. There are times when he comes and, like a lonely friend, procures a traveling companion. Luckily, this time, he treated your friend like an enemy and decided to travel his road alone."

Ptolemy went into the bedroom, the whiskey bottle in hand. Maine lay on the bed, his arm wrapped in white linen. His face was near unrecognizable, as swollen as it was.

"It seems you are unkillable," said Ptolemy, uncorking the bottle. "And that you are all you claim to be."

"And more," said Maine, taking the offered bottle.

Ptolemy had to laugh.

Maine, though it made him wince, laughed too. "Sarah?"

"Rode on without me."

"I am sorry to hear that. Seemed you two might have made a pair."

"We did," said Ptolemy. "Maybe we will again."

"You'll be heading back to Abilene, I suspect. Back to your son and employer."

"Next train out. I will return home, where I will have to explain how I failed in so many ways. Failed to hire the hands, failed to protect them from Gramm. Failed to hold on to what might have been. . ." he paused. "What might have been."

"Or what might be," said Maine. "Life is not sands in an hourglass; it is the choices we make on a long road to meeting our death. You keep doing your work, loving your boy, helping. And failing and failing and failing toward what I can see in you to be the vision of a greater victory. I have lived the second half of my life entirely preoccupied with being the best, Mr. Ptolemy. The best," he said, the word so sharp and clear. "And before I met you, being best meant one thing. And now, after you. . . consider my opinion transformed."

"I find no issue with that opinion, Mr. Maine," he said, placing a hand on Maine's shoulder. "No issue at all."

"You saved my life." Maine lifted the bottle to his lips but did not drink. "Here's to many more victories against Ol' Grim." He toasted.

And passing the bottle back and forth and back and forth, they drank together.

About the Author

C.S. Humble is the award-winning American novelist of the Amid the Vastness of All Else Saga. He is also a screenplay and short story writer. He lives in East Texas.

A Note from Shortwave Publishing

Thank you for reading *San Antonio Mission*! If you enjoyed this book, please consider writing a review. Reviews help readers find more titles they may enjoy, and that helps us continue to publish titles like this.

For more Shortwave titles, visit us online. . .

OUR WEBSITE
shortwavepublishing.com

SOCIAL MEDIA
@ShortwaveBooks

EMAIL US
contact@shortwavepublishing.com